Second Chance at Love ®

CAN'T SAY NO

JEANNE GRANT

Second Chance at Love books are published by
The Berkley Publishing Group
200 Madison Avenue, New York, NY 10016

"I'm not sure I like you, Hart."

"Honey." There was patience in his tone, but his voice was strained. "You've got...*maybe*...ten seconds to tell me what you want."

Bree knew exactly what he wanted to hear. She'd sent him all the yeses in body language; it wasn't enough.

"Yes," she whispered.

"Can't hear you."

"*Yes,*" she whispered more clearly.

"Can't hear you."

"Hart, I want you!" she yelled irritably. "Do I have to shout it from the rooftops?"

Hart leaned back and offered her a very quick, very wicked grin. "Yes," he whispered.

Jeanne Grant is a native of Michigan, where she and her husband own cherry and peach orchards and also grow strawberries. In addition to raising two children, she has worked as a teacher, counselor, and personnel manager. Jeanne began writing at age ten. She's an avid reader as well, and says, *"I don't think anything will ever beat a good love story."*

Dear Reader:

June is busting out all over, and this month's SECOND CHANCE AT LOVE romances are filled with the warmth, humor, and originality you look for.

In *The Steele Trap* (#268) by Betsy Osborne, Kerry O'Kaye comes to a romance convention with her best friend, who's written a perfectly dreadful romance, and unintentionally wins the hero as a door prize! You'll love this delightfully updated Cinderella tale, in which a sweet kindergarten teacher spends a weekend with princely Steele Gray, a devastating man-about-town, and finds her happily-ever-after ending — of course!

Carole Buck makes Shakespeare as accessible as a SECOND CHANCE AT LOVE romance in *Love Play* (#269). With wit and sparkle she captures wonderfully eccentric British characters, creates magical kingdoms onstage, and adds a dash of "rosemary for remembrance"! And all the while she brings a lovably bluestocking heroine together with such a mouth-watering hero, you'll surely be swept away. Watch especially for the marvelous reconciliation scene — it's smashing!

In *Can't Say No* (#270), Jeanne Grant creates a heroine who literally can't speak until halfway through the book! Does it work? You bet! But that's not all. Don't miss what happens when Bree spies the hero, Hart Manning, through her telescope, entertaining a series of women in his bedroom! Or when her strait-laced parents arrive unexpectedly to find clothes strewn across the yard! Such goings-on can only hint at the boisterous humor and heartfelt poignancy of this wonderfully satisfying read.

In *A Little Night Music* (#271) by Lee Williams, ad executive Kathy Groves has *two* suitors. One is seductive Jonathan Woods, the classical-music disc jockey she intends to make a household name. The other is the roommate she's never seen, whose endearingly proper wooing becomes gradually more risqué. Lee Williams's snappy dialogue and zany scenes, as well as her familiarity with the music world (after all, she's written the score for an off-off-Broadway play, toured as a rock star, *and* composed songs for well-known pop singers) fill *A Little Night Music* with zest and energy.

Have you ever felt better suited to a nineteenth-century lady's life of leisure than to a twentieth-century woman's fight for independence? If so, *A Bit of Daring* (#272) by Mary Haskell will shed new light — and laughter — on your dilemma. Melinda Pelham is the quintessential hothouse flower who fights her "old-fashioned" tendencies by striving to be the "thoroughly modern Mellie" she thinks dashing Jonathan King wants. Once again Mary Haskell provides heartwarming insight into the stickier aspects of contemporary loving.

When a romance author writes about a heroine who's a stripper, as Jan Mathews did in *Slightly Scandalous* (#226), she's got a tough act to follow. Jan does so superbly in *Thief of Hearts* (#273) — by pairing another kooky but endearing heroine with a hero of traditional values and rock-solid temperament. After Wade meets Candy, his life is never quite the same! Crazy incidents abound in this out-of-the-ordinary romance, but as always, Jan has a serious message to convey as well — and she tells it with powerful effectiveness.

I hope you enjoy reading all six SECOND CHANCE AT LOVE romances as much as we've enjoyed working on them. Until next month, happy reading!

With warm wishes,

Ellen Edwards

Ellen Edwards, Senior Editor
SECOND CHANCE AT LOVE
The Berkley Publishing Group
200 Madison Avenue
New York, N.Y. 10016

CAN'T
SAY NO

Chapter One

"Bree, eventually your speech will come back. The battery of tests proved there's nothing physically wrong." Dr. Willming leaned forward, peering at her through thick lenses. "The mind has curious ways of dealing with traumatic shock. You'll talk again, I promise you, sweetheart. Just accept that your body is asking for a little rest right now—and we both know you could use a lesson or two on how to take it easy, now don't we?"

He'd worked so hard for a smile that Bree had to give him one. It was genuine, actually. She'd known the white-haired physician half her life and loved him to bits. And having seen more doctors than she cared to count over the last few weeks, she still valued Dr. Willming's opinion most. Lowering her eyes to mask the frustration that was pictured there, she reached down for her purse.

"Bree, it would help a great deal if you'd get it through your pretty head that you were *not* responsible for your grandmother's death," the doctor continued in that low, vibrant voice of his. "You *know* her heart had been weak for years, and you *know* that no one could have done anything to prevent what happened. Now, I want you to get some solid rest and put a few hefty pounds under your belt."

Bree glanced first at the doctor's ponderous belly and then at her own slim, belted form. At Dr. Willming's irrepressible chuckle, she felt her own lips twitch. Five

1

minutes later, she escaped the good doctor's fiftieth round of reassurances—after an affectionate hug—and let herself out into the long corridor between offices. Her leather heels clicked a staccato rhythm on the shiny linoleum, slowing only when she stepped outside and faced a flat gray rain.

Maybe there was another city as ugly as South Bend at winter's end and in the middle of a downpour, but Bree doubted it. By the time she climbed into her car, water was dribbling down the nape of her neck, her hair was slicked to her scalp, and even her eyelashes were dripping. Shivering, she jabbed the key into the ignition, started the engine, and then, for no reason at all, leaned back in the seat and shut her eyes.

Dr. Willming had been coddling her for two weeks. Bree wanted to feel grateful, and instead was inclined to pull out her hair. Being treated like spun sugar was exhausting. Actually, she'd always thought of herself as a little more of the lemon than the meringue.

And this business about a "traumatized speech loss" was nonsense. Obviously, what she had was a temporarily loose screw. Bree was instinctively compassionate with other people's weaknesses and problems, but she'd never had an ounce of patience for her own. There was clearly nothing physically wrong with her; she'd never once flipped out in a crisis; a ton of people counted on her being dependable...

The engine coughed. Bree opened her eyes, shoved the car in gear, and backed out of the parking space. A half-hour later, she parked in her apartment's lot and noted, without surprise, that it was raining even harder than it had been when she left Dr. Willming's office. She made a mad dash for the door.

Inside, the gloomy day spilled in through her living-room windows. Switching on a lamp, she unbuttoned her raincoat. Absently, her eyes roved over the furnishings she'd so painstakingly chosen a few years before, all creams and cocoas and browns—the neutral shades that had then been so popular.

Two weeks ago, she'd discovered that neutral, soothing colors drove her bananas.

But that's only because you've turned into a moody, spoiled brat, Bree wryly informed herself, and swept past the offending decor, striding toward the bedroom for her brush. A headache nagged at her temples, the same stupid headache that had dogged her every step for the last two weeks.

She wandered to the window, staring out mindlessly. Her entire world seemed to be crashing down around her, for no good reason. Gram's death had been the catalyst; still, it wasn't just the trauma of loss, but also that suddenly she was seeing everything through Gram's eyes. Her fiancé, Richard, for instance. If she'd had a few secret doubts about marrying him before this, she'd tried to ignore them. Richard was affectionate and smart and thoughtful and nice looking; what more could a woman want in a man? Gram had labeled him "Sweet, Bree," the afternoon she'd met him, and pursed her lips as she'd made herself a cup of tea, only later adding absently, "Did you ever stop to think that even a molasses cookie can have too much molasses?"

It was all too rare finding a man with a "sweet" side; Bree hadn't listened to Gram. However, she'd done nothing *but* listen to Richard since this business of not being able to talk. Good Lord, the man was happy extolling the merits of computer systems for hours at a stretch. Rationally, of course, Bree should have found the subject fascinating. She herself was a systems analyst, having chosen that field because it offered women good opportunities for promotion as well as more than adequate salaries.

"And you're bored silly," Gram used to say. "Don't you remember that as a little girl, the only thing you ever wanted to do was make perfumes when you grew up?

What happened to the dreams, Bree?"

Dreams didn't pay the rent. Bree's salary from Marie paid the rent. Bree's eyes focused on the stack of computer printouts on her dresser, provided free of charge by her boss on the premise that work would get Bree's mind off her "little problem." Marie was incredibly talented at manipulating people, but she smiled and complimented so often that being used by her seemed like a privilege. "Baggage," Gram had labeled Marie. "A clever bit of baggage; take off the paint and she's all tough leather." Bree hadn't listened to her; Gram couldn't possibly understand what it took for a woman to survive in today's business world. If the little exploitations were endless, Marie still paid well and had given her every opportunity to advance. Bree had never been too unhappy.

She was just unhappy now. During the last few weeks, everything seemed to bother her, and trailing her like a shadow had been a ridiculous, irresponsible, unforgivable urge just to pitch it all.

Bree gnawed at her lip, thinking of Gram, until a thin film of tears filled her eyes. She blinked back the tears, and when her vision cleared she found herself staring at the half open door of her closet. The edge of one suitcase peeked out at her, and she had a sudden, very inviting image of herself unpacking that suitcase in the South Carolina woods, in the loft of an extremely rustic log cabin, with Gram's things around her and no telephone and absolutely nothing intruding on her peace...

"Bree, I simply can't let you do this, darling." Addie Penoyer trailed her daughter through the airport lobby, dodging suitcases and squalling children and yawning businessmen. "It just isn't like you to behave so impetuously. Honey, you can't possibly cope with a trip like this. Look how difficult it was for you to even buy the ticket."

Someone in the bustling crowd jostled Addie; Bree protectively grabbed her mother's arm with a frown and glanced up frantically as the loudspeaker announced her flight.

"I *wish* you would listen to me," Addie wailed. "Richard called us last night, after he saw you. Bree, you can't be serious about breaking off the engagement. And Marie—honey, she just can't believe you'd leave her in the lurch like this. She said she'd just taken on two new clients that only you could handle; you know how much she thinks of you, darling. All of us understand that you're not yourself right now, but..."

Bree had intended to navigate the airport alone, but that had turned into one of those best laid plans of mice and men. Her mother had been convinced that Bree couldn't handle the tickets and luggage and car rental arrangements on her own. Unfortunately, Addie had been proved right, and Bree was already frazzled. She had learned, to her sorrow, how ineffectively scratch paper and pen communicated in a world of talkers. And her mother's continuous barrage of reproachful pressure wasn't helping an already thundering headache.

With an arm around Addie's shoulder, Bree determinedly steered her toward the terminal entrance. "This just isn't right," Addie continued distractedly. "All alone in that cabin... I'm going to talk to your father again; that's what I'm going to do."

"Mom, I'll be fine," Bree mouthed firmly. "Please don't worry."

"Pardon?"

Bree sighed. Her lips formed "I love you, Mom," and then tightened anxiously as she heard her flight called a second time.

"Well, at *least* promise me you'll take care of yourself."

Bree nodded vigorously four times and offered yet another warm, reassuring hug. *Mothers.* A moment later,

Addie was safely out the door, and Bree dodged a pair of howling twins in a frantic dash for her plane. By the time she reached her flight's waiting room, her heart was tripping in double time and her nerves felt like tumbling Tinkertoys. "You're the last one," the blond stewardess told her cheerfully. "Have a good flight, now."

Bree nodded, answering her with an automatic half-smile. Inside the plane, another stewardess wanted to see Bree's ticket, and as she groped in her shoulder bag for it she caught her reflection in the small rectangular mirror on the opposite wall. At least the woman staring back at her didn't look like a wild lady with a screw loose.

Shoulder-length auburn hair, glossy and thick, framed small, delicate features. The chin was a little stubborn, but the green eyes were huge and downright beautiful . . . and makeup had done wonders for the circles beneath them. Maybe her skin looked a little oddly pale, but the cream silk blouse and tan linen skirt presented a crisply attractive image. She had the most beautiful smile this side of the moon, her father always told her. That was nice. At the moment, her legs felt as strong as tapioca and her stomach was growling with nerves, but at least those kinds of things didn't show.

"Down four rows, Ms. Penoyer . . ." The stewardess directed her with a smile, handing back her ticket.

Gratefully, Bree stepped forward. All she wanted was her assigned seat, a pillow, and silence. Obviously, freedom was getting to her, she thought wryly. She was now without a fiancé, without a job— heck, without a future. It *had* proved a little tiring to tear up her entire life in a matter of days. Actually, it was going to take every last bit of energy she could dredge up to get to Gram's cabin, but that goal beckoned like sunlight after days of rain. If she could only be done with this night flight and just *be there* . . .

She paused in the aisle next to her assigned window seat. To get to it, she was going to have to maneuver herself past an incredibly long pair of stretched-out legs. The man was dead-to-the-world asleep, precisely the activity Bree had in mind for herself, but in the meantime he was one more roadblock in an incredibly long week of them.

She bent over him and tried to whisper, "Excuse me." Unfortunately, no sound escaped her lips. *When* was she going to get used to that? Exasperated with herself, she sighed, and pitched her shoulder bag over the man to her seat. He didn't budge.

She wasn't surprised. One glance told her she wasn't going to like him. Normally, she took her time about judging people, but this man was such an easy read. He was all the things that got a woman in trouble. His thick sweep of sun-bleached hair was disheveled, Robert Redford style. He had classic, good-looking features and barely a character line, though he must have been more than thirty. His skin was suntanned, out of season. The body was long; the shoulders would have made a linebacker jealous; and Bree had always had a low tolerance for Adonises. In the meantime, his macho Italian tailoring was still blocking her path.

She touched his shoulder, which accomplished nothing. An explosion clearly wouldn't wake him. Frustrated, she tried to climb over him modestly, but her straight linen skirt would only spread so far. Muttering under her breath, she hiked up her skirt and lifted her leg to take the classic Mother-May-I giant step.

The passenger in front chose that instant to propel his seat back. Bree jolted forward, grappling for balance, and instantly felt two hands reach out to assist her, one curling intimately around her hip and the other splaying on her ribs. The contact couldn't have lasted ten seconds, ten seconds in which her shocked eyes locked with a pair of dark, dark blue ones. His weren't looking at her face but at the open throat of her silk blouse. It wasn't his fault that her breasts were all but mashed in his face, but no one, Bree thought irritably, had the right to wake up that fast.

"You're all right?"

Awkwardly, she tumbled the rest of the way into her seat, and then patiently stared at the big brown hand that seemed to have parked itself on her thigh. The hand lifted. Slowly. Nodding distantly in answer to the man's question, she bent her head to strap herself in. She had to fumble with the seat belt, of course. Talk about a sea of troubles. And the moment she was settled, a frigid draft wafted down from the little air vent above her head. She reached up to adjust the vent, but had obviously just penned herself in.

With an amused smile, her seatmate reached up and moved the air vent for her. "Better?" he asked.

She nodded again. Seconds later, the plane's engines vibrated into motion. Bree stared out the window at the dark night with its peppering of airport lights, but was well aware the passenger next to her was blatantly checking out the territory. Her breasts were receiving a second approving inspection, she was delighted to know. When he reached down for a magazine, he also gave her legs a four-star rating, and he forgot the magazine on the way back up. When those navy eyes of his concentrated even longer on her face, she could feel a ridiculous heat climbing up her cheeks.

Why me? she thought glumly. Why couldn't God's gift to women have settled in the smoking section?

"Are you flying farther than Charlotte?" he asked conversationally.

She shook her head no, trying to make the motion chilly and dismissing. Even his voice annoyed her; it was one of those husky, sexy baritones. She closed her eyes, ignoring him.

"Do you want me to get you a pillow?" he continued blithely. "I'll probably sleep through the flight myself. I've been traveling for more than thirty-six hours."

Unwillingly, her eyes blinked open again, and unfortunately his were there waiting for her—dark blue and suggestive of satin sheets and accomplished seduction techniques. His lips broke into a wonderful smile at having won her attention.

"Hart Manning here." He extended his hand.

For the sake of politeness, Bree offered him her hand. His grip was firm and warm and—as expected—lingered far too long. His thumb brushed her wrist in a way that promised limitless sensual potential. Yawning, Bree tucked her hand back in her lap where it was much safer, resisted the urge to fasten the neck button of her blouse, and stared with annoyance at her skirt, which had ridden up above her knees. To push the thing down would be like admitting he was getting to her.

"You didn't say if you wanted a pillow."

All she really wanted was for him to shut up. She shook her head.

"Is there some reason you're not talking? " he asked, his tone throaty with amusement. "Or maybe your name's a deep, dark secret? It's a long flight, you know."

And getting longer. Luckily, the stewardess paused in front of them, diverting her seatmate's attention. Actually, the two appeared mutually diverted. The brunette was savoring Mr. Manning as if she'd just discovered chocolate. "I'll be serving snacks in just a bit. Would either of you like a drink in the meantime?"

Bree's throat was parched. She parted her lips simply to ask for water . . . and then wearily closed them. No more. She'd already been totally mortified at the ticket counter, trying to talk via pad and pen. Once she was alone at Gram's cabin, the squirrels wouldn't care that she was as mute as a stone, but for now she just couldn't handle any more complications.

"Scotch for me," her seatmate said smoothly, but instead of looking at the stewardess he was studying Bree. A ripple of a frown dipped into his tanned forehead.

He said nothing until the stewardess returned with his drink. "The lady has changed her mind and would like a scotch as well," he told her.

"Certainly, sir." The brunette beamed.

Bree glowered. She hated scotch. Furthermore, Mr. Manning refused to stop staring at her. Averting her face, she again tried to ignore him.

"There you go . . ." Hart pulled down the tray in front of her, set her unwanted drink on it, and arranged the napkin. His movements were so casual and automatic that she was totally unprepared for his next one. Firm fingers claimed her chin and tilted her face to his. "I didn't mean to offend by teasing you before," he said quietly. "I didn't realize that you couldn't speak. Look . . . I know how difficult it can be for you in public; I have a second cousin who's deaf. And if I could help . . ."

He enunciated in clear, careful tones. Ideal for a lip reader. Frustration warred in Bree with an unfamiliar confusion. Something was wrong with her pulse rate. Something that directly related to the caress of his forefinger on her cheek.

His fingers gradually dropped, and she groped for the drink, taking a quick gulp. The scotch was awful, awful, awful. Like oil. Still, she took another slow sip before setting the glass down again. Immediately, those fingers reached for her chin again, as firmly determined as they were gentle, forcing her eyes to meet his.

"Are you still offended? I really didn't mean to tease you," he repeated softly. He stared at the trace of moisture on her bottom lip as if he'd just found gold. Wet gold. A wickedly elusive smile touched his mouth. "But you're also an exceptionally attractive woman. You can hardly blame me for coming on to you. And believe me, whether or not you can talk doesn't make a whit of difference."

Very slowly, she removed those long fingers from her chin, replaced them in his lap, and bent down to get the

notepad and pen from her purse. Her thumb clicked down
the ball point with a vengeance. "Mr. Manning," she
wrote swiftly, "I am neither deaf nor desperate. Lay off
and we'll get along just fine."

She handed him the scribbled sheet. He burst out
laughing. Not the response she was expecting. Several
passengers glanced in their direction, and Bree flushed
with embarrassment. Hart Manning's eyes danced back
tangos of amusement. "But you can't talk? Don't tell me
I misunderstood that."

She nodded.

"Since you were young?" His voice was gentle with
empathy.

She shook her head no. Wearily. Wasn't he getting
tired yet?

"You've been ill, then," he probed quietly. "A recent
operation?"

She shook her head again.

"It isn't physical? But then..." An absent frown
puckered his forehead. "Why?"

He had just that kind of voice; one wanted to tell him
everything—dark secrets, buried guilts, indecent fan-
tasies. Bree bet a lot of women had mistaken the timbre
of that seductive baritone for sympathy. She had already
figured out that the man was downright nosy.

Unfastening her seat belt, she curled a leg under her,
leaned back against the headrest, and closed her eyes.
She was going to sleep if it killed her.

Naturally, instant sleep proved impossible. She felt as
relaxed as a drummer in a parade. Yes, she was a thirty-
year-old woman who had certainly handled her share of
men. But Hart Manning still made her unreasonably
nervous. Verbal defenses had always been her specialty;
she felt a horrible vulnerability without them. And he
was still looking at her. She could sense his curiosity;
she had the terrible feeling he was the kind of man who
never left a puzzle until every last piece was in place.

He almost made her feel...afraid. Which was ridiculous. What was there to be afraid of?

Ten minutes later, Bree opened her eyes to see the stewardess removing their drinking glasses. "He went out like a light, didn't he?" the brunette whispered with a little laugh.

Bree nodded, regarding her seatmate with a dry half-smile. His eyes were closed, his legs stretched out, and he was clearly enjoying the deep sleep of the just.

So much for the hunt and chase, and that foolish little frisson of fear. Mr. Manning had never been a danger, anyway, not to Bree. She could take care of herself; she always had. She'd work herself out of this no-talk non-sense and get back to managing her life...

And what a tremendous job you've been doing of that lately, Bree, a small voice whispered in her head.

Bree sighed, suddenly feeling a mixture of depression and confusion. Closing her eyes, she curled up toward the window—as far away from her seatmate as possible—and fell asleep.

Chapter Two

THE MENTAL PICTURES were so vivid to Bree that they never seemed part of a dream. It was just . . . happening again.

Charcoal clouds drooped low, and snow pitched down helter-skelter. Bree curled a protective arm around the diminutive shoulders of her grandmother, and squeezed. "I don't believe I let you talk me into taking you out in this weather," she scolded.

"Couldn't stand to be cooped up another minute. What a winter this has been!" Gram chuckled, her pale blue eyes nestled in a sea of soft, wrinkled skin. "We bought out the stores, didn't we, Bree? Haven't a penny left in my purse." Her lips compressed as Bree gradually stole two more packages from the armful Gram was toting. "What do you think I am, helpless? I can carry my own load just fine. Don't *you* start treating me like a senile old woman who has to be humored."

"All right. You want to carry all your packages and mine, too? Just to prove you're a tough old cookie?" Bree asked.

"*Old?* Eighty-five isn't old. Now ninety—ninety starts getting up there."

Bree laughed, casting a loving glance at her tiny grandmother. Tenacious, sassy, and fiercely independent—that was Gram, who stubbornly denied her failing health, who drank sherry with her peppermint ice cream, who had spurred Bree into every mischievous escapade she'd ever been on. Often Bree thought that Gram wished her granddaughter had been just a little bit more... wicked. More interesting. More prone to trouble. As Gram had been in *her* youth. Bree had always had a boring tendency to be good.

At the moment, she had a definite inclination to get Gram out of the snow and wind. "Now just wait here," Bree ordered her, as she grabbed the rest of the packages and settled Gram under the sheltering canopy of a department store entrance. "I'll bring the car around in two seconds flat."

In four minutes flat, she pulled up to the store, her mind more on fixing Gram's supper than on standing in a no-parking zone. Hats bobbed, blocking her view; she stepped out of the car, intending to motion to her grandmother. Bodies seemed to be deliberately obscuring her vision, and a tiny frown flickered across her brow.

And then someone moved, and there was Gram, clutching her purse as a stranger tried to grab it. Gram, shouting, her little gray topknot all awry, her gentle features contorted, and Bree was suddenly running, running...

She managed to get her hands on the thief; her head cracked when he slammed her against a concrete wall as he made his escape. There was blood on her scalp; she could feel it, but worse than that was the crowd, where curious blank faces surrounded her as she surged frantically toward her grandmother.

A man in a navy uniform tried to shield her from the small prone body... as if anyone could possibly keep her away from Gram! Bree threw herself down, feeling her knee scrape raw through slushy cement, not caring, not believing the terrible blue-gray color of Gram's lips, the way she was clutching her heart. "I'm afraid it's a heart attack, miss," someone said, and Bree said fiercely, *"No!"*

Gram's face was ashen, her hand far too cool and weak in Bree's. "The cabin," Gram whispered. "It's for you, Bree, when you need it. Remember..."

"You'll be *fine*," Bree said desperately. "Don't talk, Gram. Don't..."

"Fight for what you want, darlin'," Gram said. "Nothing halfway. Don't you settle for halfway, Bree..."

Nothing could have hurt more than that machete slash of pain as Gram smiled one last time. The whine of a siren in the distance became a shriek, augmented by a terrible silent scream in Bree's head that no one else could hear...

"Wake up. *Now,* honey." Bree's eyes flew open as a strong hand shook her shoulder and a pair of intense navy-blue eyes fastened on her own. For a moment, she was totally disoriented to see a stranger's face peering at her with such fierce concern, but then she recognized Hart Manning. And before she was fully awake, his lips had curled into an immediately relaxed smile. "Whether you know it or not, sweetheart, there isn't a thing wrong with your vocal cords. You can scream like a banshee— in fact, you just did, in your sleep. And since you've deprived us both of any possible rest, you may as well buckle up. We're landing."

Bree's lips parted to deliver a rejoinder, failed to produce any sound, and formed a thin line to stop their trembling. Tears had collected in her eyes during the dream; she blinked them back, ducking her head to fumble with the seat belt—only to find she was draped from neck to toes in a blanket.

With a frown, she pushed the thing aside, not remembering when the blanket or the pillow behind her had appeared. For a moment, she couldn't think at all but could only feel. Her emotions bounced from the guilt she felt for her grandmother's death to her relief at being jolted from the endlessly recurring nightmare to...rage at the insensitive clod next to her.

Rage won out. Furiously, she fastened her seat belt. *Hart,* was it? Well, anyone with any *heart* would have at least offered her a little sympathy after a terrifying nightmare...

Of course, if he had, you would have burst into tears and embarrassed yourself no end, her mind's voice swiftly reminded her.

"And we'd better finish putting you back together, honey..."

If there was anything Bree hated, it was someone who tossed out casual endearments like *honey.* After glaring up into a pair of fathomless blue eyes, she lowered her gaze and glimpsed her bone pumps, swinging back and forth from his finger. She snatched them, not remembering having removed her shoes any more than she remembered the appearance of the blanket and pillow.

A watery sun was peering through the tiny plane window, and Bree's stomach went bump as the earth seemed to rush up at them. She put her shoes on, then hurriedly grabbed her purse and reached in for a brush and compact. What she needed was a bathroom and some soap and water; her compact mirror affirmed that three hours' sleep hadn't been nearly enough. Her makeup had long ago worn off; dark, bruised eyes and tousled hair confronted her, along with lips gnawed red in the process of reliving Gram's death.

From the corner of the mirror, she glimpsed her seatmate's expression. Her hasty brush strokes stopped. He was... staring. And the corners of his lips were just turned up, as if he'd caught her doing something intimate.

"You have someone to help you at the airport?" he asked.

Ignoring him, Bree shoved the brush back in her purse and hurriedly stood up, in a sudden rush to get off the plane, which had taxied to a stop. Hart stayed right behind her; she knew, because she could feel those navy eyes riveted on her back. And like a schoolgirl, she was conscious of bra straps showing through the silk of her blouse, of every motion of her hips . . . *darn* it. Did her fanny sway or jiggle or bounce or whatever when she walked? She hadn't worried about such idiotic things in years.

She forgot him for an instant as she stepped off the plane and climbed down the metal boarding ramp. Sultry heat assaulted her in dizzying, shimmering waves, and the early morning sun was almost enough to burn her eyes. Still, she could smell the mountains. A three-hour drive and she'd be in the Appalachians; there'd be woods and silence, and the trillium would just be starting to bloom. There was no softer solace than Gram's feather bed . . .

Still, her fingertips touched her temples once she entered the main airport terminal. Frigid air conditioning chilled her skin; there was such terrible noise and confusion, and her heartbeat picked up the cadence of anxiety. Everything would be fine once she got to the cabin, but around people she felt isolated by an invisible glass wall, knowing she couldn't communicate.

"So there *isn't* anyone waiting for you. I should have guessed," Hart said disgustedly.

She looked up, unaware he was still behind her until she felt his hand resting possessively on the small of her back, redirecting her steps to the right instead of the left.

"The baggage pickup is this way. You have to read the signs. You do read?" he asked conversationally. "First impressions are deceiving. I had you pegged for the efficient, self-sufficient type, if you want to know the truth. Now, do you think you can possibly cope from here?"

Depression didn't stand a chance next to a healthy, invigorating surge of rage. Four-letter words tripped on her tongue, fell back, and stuck helplessly somewhere in her throat. "Yes," her lips formed frigidly. "I can cope just fine. Leave me alone, would you?"

"Can't understand you. You've got an arousing pair of . . . lungs, honey. Why don't you use them?"

He stalked off through the throng of people waiting for luggage. Anxiety faded in Bree, replaced by a second wind of energy. Furious energy. For two cents, she would have followed him and landed a right hook . . . but then, she wasn't the type. She had no temper now and never had. "Bree's my good one," her mother used to say. "I can always count on her to stay cool and calm; she never even cried as a baby . . ."

Good Bree, good Bree, echoed the rollicking headache in her temples. An arousing pair of lungs, was it? Bristling, she stalked toward the luggage pickup. Lungs, schmungs. The first time she'd laid eyes on Hart, she'd guessed he was obsessed with that particular portion of a woman's anatomy. You could always spot a breast man in a crowd.

Richard, being a *decent* man, would never have been so crude as to stare at any woman below the neck.

Richard would also have helped her with her luggage, instead of leaving her standing there, the last one in the crowd, to face a moving conveyer with nothing on it. *Where* were her two pale blue suitcases?

The attendant looked blank. After two phone calls and seven pieces of paper from Bree's scratch pad, she gathered that her luggage was on some other plane. Apologies and promises were politely delivered . . . one day, at most two, hand-delivered to her doorstep . . .

Which was nice. Except that her silk blouse was already wrinkled and damp with perspiration, and her pencilslim skirt was hardly cabin attire. Glumly, Bree stalked off in search of her rental car, her stomach starting to cramp from hunger and her muscles protesting too many nights of insufficient rest.

She became abruptly alert as she neared the rent-a-car desk. Hart Manning was there, bent over the long counter as he filled out some forms, his leonine mane unmistakable. He *certainly* wasn't delivering sarcastic comments to the clerk as he had to Bree. The blonde was laughing, all dimples and bright blue eyes.

Ducking behind a conveniently tall businessman, Bree bolted for the farthest clerk as she rapidly smoothed her blouse and flicked back her hair. On the off-chance Hart should look her way, she'd make certain that the egotistical, opinionated boor saw a—how had he put it?— an efficient, self-sufficient woman. Her smile was wide awake and brilliantly capable as the young redheaded man across the counter glanced up, indicating it was her turn.

"How you doin', miss?" The clerk had a cheeky grin and a wink for a hello. "What can I do for you?" It took several seconds for him to readjust his eyes down from her face to the piece of paper her hand was frantically waving. "Bree Penoyer, a month's car rental, huh? Okay, sweets..."

But he returned a moment later with a boyish shrug. "You sure it's under that name?"

She nodded vigorously.

"Can't find a thing."

"Already paid for it, you must," she scribbled rapidly on her pad, but he'd turned to answer another customer's question, and he didn't see the note. He just winked again in her direction. Two customers later, she regained his attention, at least insofar as he leaned on the countertop and stared at her like a lovesick calf. "Hi again."

Weren't there child labor laws in this state? The kid couldn't have been eighteen.

"My car," Bree scrawled desperately.

"Maybe it was another rental agency? You want a phone?"

A phone was as useful to her as diamonds in the desert. Tears were so ridiculously close she was ashamed of herself. She never cried. "Please look again," she scribbled, and sent pleading eyes to the young redhead.

"Hey, look, no problem. There's a convention in town, and we're booked up, but we'll get you something." The boy brought back a computer list, suggesting three gas guzzlers that would cost her twice as much as the one she had arranged for.

Bree closed her eyes in frustration, dragging one hand through her hair.

"Now what's the problem?" growled a baritone next to her.

Bree's spine turned ruler-straight, her lips twisting in a stiff smile. "Nothing," she mouthed to Hart.

"No problem exactly, mister..." The readhead explained the mix-up with a happy grin. That grin gradually faded as Hart let forth a stream of invective.

Fifteen minutes later, Bree had in her hand the keys to an affordable compact, and faced the nasty job of having to thank her rescuer. "Thanks," she mouthed tightly.

"Can't understand a word. I admit I'm fascinated by your game of not talking, but the immediate priority is food for the hungry. Usually, I offer a woman a meal *before* we've slept together—you're a passionate snuggler, aren't you, Bree? Or at least you *were* until you decided to start screaming. Now, now..." Hart shot her a lazy grin when her eyebrows shot up in outrage. He added in a whisper, "I had to pick up your name from the rental agent, since you're so stingy with conversation. You look like hell, you know. Actually, a lot of men would probably burn for the way you look. I fail to understand why there isn't a ring on your finger. You've been in Siberia for the last decade? Never mind. You can explain it all to me in sign language while we're eating."

A lynching, truthfully, would be too good for him. People were staring at them. Actually, it wasn't people but women, looking not at them but at *him*. He drew every feminine eye as they passed, with his nauseating Greek-god profile and commanding stride. Furthermore, he was actually trying to tow her along with him . . . at least until she dug in her heels at the restaurant door, shaking her head vigorously.

"I take it that's supposed to mean no? Honey, I've heard more noes that mean yes from women than there's honey in a beehive. I watched you the entire time you were racing around the airport—and we both know you're in no shape to drive. You could barely keep your eyes open getting off the plane, and your stomach was grumbling half the night. *And* you have a headache, don't you?"

She shook her head in denial.

He tapped her nose gently with his forefinger. "And you're a fibber. Amazing how a woman can fib without even talking."

An hour later, Bree climbed into her rental car, locked the doors, checked the locks on all the doors, started the engine, and jammed her foot on the accelerator. The weariness and depression that had been following her like a shadow these last weeks were gone. Every cell in her body was vibrating with life, after an incredible hour of that man staring at her over a restaurant table. He hadn't been happy until she'd eaten ham, sausage, eggs, and hash browns with two cups of coffee . . . She *never* ate that kind of breakfast.

Nor had she ever met a pushier, nosier man than Hart Manning. The less she answered his questions, the more he looked as if he'd gotten hold of a priceless puzzle that increasingly intrigued him. And he'd almost—once— made her laugh, with his coaxing grin and irreverent humor. She'd stopped herself in time. A woman should never encourage a stranger, and she could guess his intentions from the way he kept looking at her, at her breasts and throat and eyes . . . it was nerve-racking. The man was probably in heat constantly. She'd had a cat like that once.

She'd gotten rid of the cat.

A car zoomed past her, and she flicked her eyes in the rearview mirror. And blinked. A navy-blue New Yorker was just behind her, and the driver had a leonine mane, eyes that matched his car, and a large, powerful hand that waved, all friendly-like.

Swiftly, her eyes returned to the road. Not that she could exactly accuse him of following her—he'd happily volunteered his own destination as a vacation cabin in the town just short of hers. That was still no excuse for his edging behind her as though she needed a caretaker. Her foot snapped down on the accelerator. So she looked sleepy, did she?

An hour earlier she could have fallen asleep in Grand Central Station, but now, thanks to that . . . *bully*, she couldn't have been less tired.

And as for looking like hell . . . hurriedly, she glanced at the mirror again, only to see that she might look a *little* tired, but hardly comatose. Her hair was lustrous and shiny, her skin clear, her green eyes snapping with energy, and she'd taken care of those little circles with makeup in the rest room. There was nothing wrong with the way she looked. Nothing.

Except for the delicate frown between her brows when she saw the flashing yellow light trailing her. Pulling over, Bree stopped the engine, took several deep, calming breaths, opened the window, and faced the policeman.

"Going fifteen miles over by the clock. License and registration, please."

Mortified, Bree hurriedly complied. She'd never in her life received a speeding ticket. The gentleman in the tan uniform was more than happy to educate her as to how it was done. Cheeks flaming, Bree accepted the oblong bit of paper and the stern admonition to control her hot-foot tendencies. Only by chance did she glance behind her.

Hart had pulled his navy New Yorker off the highway some distance behind her. He was yawning. *Yawning!*

For the next three hours, her speedometer never once bounced above fifty-five. Neither did her shadow's.

Gradually, rolling hills led to mountains, and the road began to dip and curve. Streams gushed over the hill-sides, stripes of silver where the sun hit. After a time, Bree flicked off the air conditioning and rolled down the windows. The air was sultry, but the smell of pungent woods soothed her fragile nerves.

Hart *was* following her; she'd known from the minute he deliberately drove past his turnoff. It would be so simple to get rid of him if she could talk, but handicapped as she was, she felt utterly helpless. Then again, her polite no-thank-you's had gotten rid of any number of unwanted men—but she had a feeling they wouldn't work with Hart. What would? She would have to do *something* about him. When she got to the cabin.

Not now, not yet. For now, she inhaled deeply and remembered why she had come here. There was no other place on earth like the mountains in South Carolina in April.

Clusters of trillium bubbled and tripped over the hill-sides in incredible snow-white splashes. The woods were verdant and ripe with new growth; every leaf seemed to catch the sun. Silence was part of the magic. Suddenly, there were no cars except hers and Hart's, just the soft shadows of woods, the occasional burst of secluded stream, the lush promise of shelter and privacy where no one would intrude.

The road to Gram's cabin curved down and around a valley. A very few other vacation cottages stood along the road, but all of them were hidden from sight, with

only crooked mailboxes to indicate their presence. The
ravine was just past that stand of trees, completely invisible from the road, a lush sanctuary for wildlife and
flowers, rising up a steep incline . . . Gram had loved it
so. Gram . . .

Shoving the car into first gear for the last steep climb,
Bree frowned absently, aware that she hadn't thought of
Gram in hours now, a first in how long?

Braking to a stop, she let a pent-up flow of weariness
flood her limbs as she gazed at the cabin. A shake-
shingled roof, log walls, a porch with a swing . . . Weeds
had overgrown everything, but if the place looked dis-
reputable to a civilized eye, Bree saw only happy memories. Eating warm chocolate cookies on that swing; toting
home a pailful of blackberries; wildflowers in every room;
going to sleep with the smell of that white, delicate blos-
som that grew everywhere; a bear one night — how Gram
had laughed at his antics, allaying the fears of the little
girl Bree had been. Like an ocean tide, there was a
rhythm to every minute she had spent in that cabin, the
ebb and flow of silence and contentment, the soothing
murmur of love she had so taken for granted as a child.

There was no other place she could possibly have
gone.

It was the perfect place . . .

A car door slammed behind her, jolting her from the
sleepy memories. Gnawing determinedly at the inside of
her lip, she snatched up her purse, unlocked the door,
and stepped out of the car, her heels sinking into the
weedy, pungent earth.

"Who on earth would have guessed you were such a
country girl?" Hart's eyes interestedly traveled the length
of her, as if he hadn't inspected her a dozen times already.
"The mystery deepens, doesn't it, Bree? I'd say you were
a man after my own heart, but one look at you and a
fool would know how inappropriate that statement would
be." His head whipped around as he jammed his hands

in his pockets. "Looks like the place has been closed up for a few years."

Those blue eyes suddenly seared hers, and she could have sworn she glimpsed an unbelievable sensitivity, even protectiveness, in them.

"So what exactly are we going to do about you, honey?" Hart murmured.

Bree made several adequate sign-language motions, indicating he could drop himself and his car into the nearest ravine.

He ignored her energetic hand signals. "I've always been happy with the place I rent, but you've really cornered a special little valley here. Any cottages for rent close by?"

She shook her head vigorously from side to side.

"I saw quite a few signs on the road—"

Violently, her head whipped back and forth again.

"Nobody's lived in that cabin for ages, I'll bet," Hart remarked conversationally.

She nodded yes, someone had. Another lie.

"Fascinating, how you can fib without even opening your mouth." Hart shook his head. "I was positive there'd be someone waiting here for you—and there's no one," he said unbelievingly. "You just decided to take off for here, looking like a model for an urban magazine, playing some game about not talking, coping as well as a lost toddler in a circus . . . I don't know why I'm asking this, but do you at least have food in the place?"

She nodded.

"So you don't even have a box of crackers. *Wonderful,*" he said flatly.

All of this just had to stop. Options flounced through her brain, most of them far too good for him. Nailed up by his thumbs. Boiling in oil. Tickled to death by African ants.

A *very* tiny corner of her brain acknowledged a wayward and totally incomprehensible attraction to him. Or maybe it was just that he intrigued her. Most men she knew backed off at a frown. Hart probably wouldn't back off for a bulldozer.

The vibrations warned her that he was a dangerous man, but he strode forward with an innocuous smile, hooking an arm around her shoulder before she could blink. When she failed to move forward, his arm swept down and his palm lightly tapped her fanny. She definitely stepped forward then. The sexual voltage was undeniable, and as wanted as a toothache.

"If you're going to keep up this silent act, I don't see you coping with a grocery store. Let's get you inside and make out a food list, and then you can crash. You lasted pretty well during the drive; I'll give you that. I was worried about you at the airport, but the spark is definitely back in your eyes." He paused at the door, then pushed it open.

Gram had never kept the cabin locked up. Why bother? This wasn't robber territory. There was nothing to steal.

There was also very little protection against a man who had suddenly developed an ominous scowl.

Chapter Three

HART GLARED FIRST inside the cabin, and then back at her. One hand rested loosely on his hip; the other pushed a shock of hair from his forehead as if he just couldn't take much more. His voice erupted in a throaty growl. "You're actually planning on *living* in this place? In the shape it's in? I really don't believe this."

That was it. Something clicked in Bree. She'd put up with his insensitivity over her nightmare; she'd taken his insulting comments about her cuddling sleep habits; she'd tolerated his *yawning* over the speeding ticket that was entirely his fault. But there was no way she was going to sit still and hear that *man* malign Gram's cabin. Slamming her purse on a dusty wood table, Bree unsnapped the top of her ball-point pen and bent over to scribble furiously on a notepad.

Hart was leaving, whether he knew it or not. And if he ventured one more amused comment about her inability to talk, he would leave with the iron frying pan, preferably connected to his head.

"I love it," a husky baritone announced.

Her writing hand wavered. Scowling, she glanced up.

Hart had taken his jacket off and was holding it with two fingers over one shoulder. His other hand was in his pocket, absently jangling change. The white shirt clung to his chest and wide shoulders, and the suit pants seemed

to have been purposely tailored to show off his flat rear
end and muscular legs. Everything about him shouted
sexual animal.

Rationally, she said to herself, so what? Irrationally,
there was a very stupid pulse in her throat that went *ping*
when Hart's head suddenly whipped around and his lazy
dark eyes settled in on hers.

"Everything in this place is a hundred years old or
more, isn't it?" he asked.

She nodded warily.

"It's like going back in time. You're a history buff?"

She nodded again. Hart wandered, one hand slipping
from his pocket occasionally to finger an object in the
room. "Fascinating."

Gram had lived in the cabin until two years ago, when
Bree's parents had whisked her off to a South Bend
apartment where she was close to medical facilities—
and their watchful eyes. Her home, though, had always
been here.

The cabin consisted of the main room, a loft, and a
lean-to in back. A trapper had built it some 150 years
before, and without sophisticated tools had hand-chinked
and notched the logs to make a snug fit. Gram had lath-
ered whitewash on the inside walls—Bree had helped
make that whitewash, stirring the hot lye mixture in a
kettle outside for two days in a row.

In one corner stood a functional spinning wheel and
carder; beyond it was an old oak chest with white porcelain pitcher and water basin. Behind Bree was the
cooking corner—the scarred converted dry sink, the ancient wood stove that still cooked the most delicious stew
this side of the Appalachians, the butter churn and vin-
egar barrel used to preserve eggs in the winter. A fat iron
kettle still rested on the brick hearth, so heavy a woman
could barely lift it, and Bree could well remember the
hours when wax had melted in that kettle to make can-

dles, even though the place was wired for electricity.

Gram used to say that people had lost the essence of life. That living wasn't weekends, or punching in and out at nine and five and playing the politics of promotion. That people had forgotten about the natural order of things, the laughter that no one had to pay for, the peace that you couldn't buy.

Certain things in the cabin were purely decorative; others were—or had once been—functional: the cradle that hung from the whitewashed rafters; butter molds shaped like pineapples; the hooked rug in blue and red and cream. Dried baby's breath and thyme still swayed from the ceiling...

...Covered in cobwebs. The whole place was wreathed in a half-inch layer of them. The early afternoon sunlight filtered through thick dust motes, nestled in spider webs, and sent mottled streams of yellow everywhere. Bree suddenly closed her eyes, aware of just how much work it was going to take to make the place livable again.

She was so weary she could barely move; for two cents she'd have walked out and flown back home... but then she thought of Gram. A shaft of guilt pierced Bree, familiar and painful, for failing Gram when she'd needed her. And because of all those memories of laughter and purpose and joy, Bree was going to find the energy to fix the place again. *And* to put her life back together, *and* to make herself talk...

"You don't mind if I take a look upstairs, do you, honey?"

"Wait!" Bree's lips soundlessly formed the words, but it was too late. Busybody was already ascending the narrow stairs to the loft.

Darn it, that was a private place. Some very foolish young-girl dreams were locked up there; Hart just plain didn't belong, though it would probably sound silly to vocalize her objections, even if she could. It was just...

the rope bed was in the loft, covered with a feather mattress so thick you sank into a cocoon when you lay down. Moonlight had a way of trickling over that bed when you first went to sleep, so bright you couldn't sleep but only dream—and they were always good dreams. The softness and the silver promise of night were plain old-fashioned erotic. The aphrodisiac of dew-scented flowers always wafted in through the window; the linen always smelled as if it had been softened and dried in the sun—because it had been.

A few moments later, Hart paused halfway down the stairs to close the loft's trapdoor again, then took three more steps down and perched on a step, studying her. Bree felt warmth rise in her cheeks for no reason at all ... or maybe because she was thinking about feather beds. Hart's lips curled in a perfectly wicked smile. "The place is yours?"

The lump in her throat felt thick and heavy. Yes, it was hers. Gram had left it to Bree in her will. Bree crumbled up the nasty note she had started to write, and simply penned out a plaintive, "Please. Won't you leave me alone?"

In four swift strides, Hart was down the steps and standing in front of her. He chucked her chin with two curled fingers, and his eyes searched hers fiercely. "Whatever it is, Bree, it's not that bad. *Nothing's* that bad. Don't you dare get that look in your eyes again."

His fingers dropped, as quickly as if he'd never touched her. Startled, Bree let out her breath, but Hart already had his hands jammed loosely in his pockets and was casually looking around the room again. "Guess it's time I got your groceries," he said idly. "You want to make out a list, or shall I just buy the obvious basics? How long are you planning to stay here, anyway?"

After a moment, Bree's lips formed a careful message: "Look, I don't want anything. Please just—"

"Didn't catch that. What did you say?" Hart waited. "You know," he said mildly, "I've always believed that people will walk all over you if you don't stand up and shout about what you want in life."

He picked up his jacket from the kitchen table, where he had casually draped it earlier. "I'll be back."

He closed the door behind him, but that didn't stop his arrogant words from ringing in her ears like a promise. Seething with helpless fury, Bree spotted a plate within arm's reach in the open cupboard. Gram had always hated that set of dishes, had meant to seek out more authentic crockery that would suit the cabin as soon as enough of that set broke or cracked to justify the expense. Gram was practical. At the moment, Bree didn't feel in the least practical; she felt out-of-control frustrated, and she soon sent one china plate hurtling toward the door, to shatter noisily in a thousand tiny pieces.

Shock replaced that instant silly feeling of satisfaction. For heaven's sake, she'd never thrown anything in her life. Of all the childish . . .

The door popped open again. A lazy, devilish grin was mounted on Hart's lips like a trophy. "Tch, tch. Who would have guessed you had such a temper?" He added gruffly, "You hold on to that temper until I get back, honey. Anger's a strong medicine that most people never take advantage of."

She *didn't* have a temper. And once her nonexistent temper had calmed down, Bree leaned back against the closed cabin door and viewed her dusty domain with dismay. At least Hart was gone, but in the meantime wishes weren't horses. The place wasn't going to clean itself.

Abruptly, she rolled up her sleeves, looped her hair in a rubber band, and dug in. Gram always found the energy to banish dust and dirt. She also used to say that determination was worth more than muscle. The last few weeks had been frightening for Bree, discovering how deeply and how long she'd let things just . . . happen to her. Gram's death had seemed a last unbearable crisis in a life where she'd taken too many wrong turns. She had to make it right again.

And the very simplest project, like cleaning, made her feel better from the start.

Gram's back-to-nature philosophy had not extended to sheer foolishness. The main part of the cabin was authentic 1830's, but the lean-to contained civilized goodies—an old washing machine, refrigerator, hot-water heater, and more to the present purpose, Gram's cleaning supplies. For starters, Bree plugged in the electrical appliances and took a match to the gas-run water heater. By some miracle, they all worked.

Once the hot water was pumping into the converted dry sink, she stood on the top of the kitchen table and scrubbed away cobwebs and dust. Using old newspapers, she attacked the windows. She was humming by the time she removed the dustcover from the bed and tossed it in the washer. A blue and white tablecloth made for a lively spot of color, as did the bright red rhododendron Bree uprooted from the woods and used as a potted centerpiece.

The cabin took on sparkle in direct proportion to Bree's taking on grime. She stopped once, to fill a glass with fresh, cold well water, downing it all in long gulps, and then glanced down at herself with a wry grimace. The cream silk blouse had a rip and several snags, and a stripe of dirt looked painted on one sleeve. The linen skirt might make a good rag; she'd already tossed her stockings in the trash; and she must be getting slap-happy tired, because her own dirt struck her as incredibly funny. Even her pink nail polish looked murky gray.

There was a chemical john in the lean-to, but no shower or bathtub. The only way to turn gray skin back to white was to swim in the pond in the ravine. Gram had stubbornly held that cold water never hurt anyone, and then, there was nothing softer than hair washed in lake water. As a kid, Bree had found bathing in the pond high adventure; but as the cabin shaped up and she battled with exhaustion, she didn't dare strip down and risk having Hart catch her taking a bath.

Of course, maybe he wouldn't come back. Bree clung to that hope as the minutes passed, making bargains with herself. If you clean that corner just so, he'll never show up again. If there isn't a single speck of dust on the floor, maybe he'll disappear off the face of the earth.

It couldn't have taken four hours to buy groceries; and he really couldn't possibly know what she wanted anyway. For that matter, if she took a towel and soap down to the pond, the chances of his finding her were nil. No one could see the pond from the road or the back of the house; you had to weave through woods and brush to get there. She would be perfectly safe, getting off her skin the layer of itchy grime that was starting to drive her bananas.

But she was sitting at the kitchen table when Hart walked in. A sponge bath at the sink had moved a little of the dirt around; her chin was cupped in a weary palm, and her eyes were staring resentfully at the door. Toothaches *always* came back.

"We haven't gotten over our temper, I see. Never mind, a little food will revive you." He plopped a bag of groceries down on the table in front of her, then disappeared outside for more. Bree's fingers drummed out the death march on the blue and white tablecloth as he carted in three more bags, but she didn't so much as glance at any of his purchases.

Hart shook his head sadly. "I leave an incredibly attractive woman and come back to a waif. Why do you wear you hair like that, anyway? It makes you look like a skinned rat."

The insult rolled off her back. What was one more?

"I didn't mean to be so long, but I got hung up in the real-estate office. Getting out of my lease may be a little tricky, but I think I can manage it. Fishing's darn good around here, the man told me. Finaker. Know him? Fat old coot. Beer belly the size of a watermelon, wolf teeth, itty-bitty eyes?"

Bree stared at him, determinedly keeping her expression neutral, and told herself that the corners of her mouth were *not* twitching. Even though Finaker did have itty-bitty eyes.

"You'd better like peanut butter..." Hart reached in the first bag to grab a massive jar of the stuff. "Figured you'd feel too lazy to cook, first day out. Just stay right where you are. I'll make the sandwiches and unpack the rest of the groceries."

Bree didn't flicker an eyelash.

A dozen steaks piled up on the table beside her. Steaks she couldn't possibly afford. A bag of oranges, another of apples, four containers of strawberries, four bags of oatmeal cookies, enough boxes of cornflakes for forty-seven people...

The corners of her mouth were trying to turn up again. He was just so... *awful*. Get ahold of yourself, Bree, she told herself sternly. He'll go away only if you ignore him.

But he was such a difficult man to ignore... He had this cajoling baritone and a wounded look as though she was hurting his feelings by not approving of his purchases, and she wasn't absolutely sure whether she wanted to kill him or laugh.

"I didn't want to trek any farther than Mapleville, so I was stuck with the local store in picking out some clothes for you. Underpants..." Gravely, Hart tossed three polka-dotted whimsies in her direction; they would have landed on her nose if she hadn't snatched at them. "Now, jeans—I figured you for about thirty-six around the hips. The lady said that was a size eight. These look a little long, but you can roll them up. Shoes—you have kind of big feet, don't you?" Hart glanced under the table at the two grimy feet clenched one on top of the other. "Good Lord, you certainly do. And I told the lady what a special pair of . . . lungs you had, and she came up with these . . ."

He draped three camisole-style T-shirts over the peanut-butter jar. One blue, one orange, one red. À navy sweat shirt followed.

"Now, you'll like this," Hart said confidentially. "I figured you'd need something to sleep in." With a wide grin, he unfolded a massive man's T-shirt. There was a huge fish printed on the chest; below were the printed words, IF YOU'RE LUCKY ENOUGH TO HOOK A SILENT WOMAN, REEL HER IN NICE AND SLOW.

Bree's head drooped over her folded hands. One violent shiver chased up her spine, and then her body convulsed with spasms of most unwilling, albeit silent, laughter. He was driving her absolutely nuts. She detested every single thing about him—he was pushy and cruel and insensitive and opinionated and too damned handsome for his own good.

Yet silent laughter continued to quiver helplessly through her like an ache—she'd forgotten how much it ached to really laugh. It must be that she was so darned overtired; there could be no other excuse.

A strong hand groped for her chin, forcing her face up for Hart's inspection. For an instant, she thought she saw concern written in his dark blue eyes, but laughter-tears were blurring her vision.

By the time Hart had softly brushed them from her cheeks, he wore a gloating expression, as if he'd won the lottery. "I knew you had a sense of humor hidden somewhere in those big green eyes."

Like the nosy man he was, he discovered the lean-to

and filled the refrigerator while she was trying to figure out what to do with him. Actually, she had little choice. He was jamming the food helter-skelter on the open shelves, and she was forced to trail frantically after him to prevent cans from toppling to the floor. On second thought, she grabbed her pad and paper, jotting down, "Are you crazy? I don't want any of this food." But he wouldn't look at the note, just grinned when they bumped hip to hip, and puttered around the pie safe until he discovered Gram's silverware.

He lavished peanut butter on thick slices of bread, then set a plate in front of her. He dragged a chair to the table for himself, peered in one last bag, and removed a bottle.

"Hooch," he announced. "Goes well with peanut butter. There's nothing like the local brew to clear out the cobwebs—and half of your brain cells. You're probably some prissy wine drinker—" He paused, giving her adequate time to defend herself, and then shrugged as he picked up her sandwich. "I figured. You're the type. Open up."

She would have gotten peanut butter all over her closed lips if she didn't. Her lips parted; Hart jammed in a man-sized bite of sandwich, looking very pleased with himself. She chewed rather inelegantly, having no choice, and the peanut butter sank to the base of her throat and sat there, dry and thick.

He pushed the glass of hooch in her direction. Only because she was afraid of choking on the peanut butter did she lift the glass to her lips. Swift as a cat, Hart reached over to tilt the glass a little farther, and she received a gigantic gulp of firewater that burned all the way down her throat. She glared.

Hart grinned. "Makes you sleep like a baby. Come on, now. You look middle-aged and unspeakably sanctimonious with your mouth all puckered like that.

Don't give me any moral claptrap about drinking in the middle of the day—who cares? Besides, it's late after-oon, and we both know you're going to bed after this anyway."

She jammed the glass back down on the table, eyeing him warily. Coming from Hart, references to bed made her nervous.

With a frown, he let that busy hand of his snake across the table again. A very gentle forefinger flicked at a crumb on her cheek. "You know," he said mildly, "you're an incredibly beautiful woman, even with black streaks all over your nose. I was thinking about you all the way into town. What a pleasure it would be to have a quiet woman around for a change, one who couldn't make demands, who couldn't whine about commitment, who wouldn't prattle on and on when a man was trying to think."

She choked, and had to grab the hooch again.

"I'm not sure I can get out of my lease, as I told you. Been renting the same cabin for a number of years, but that glass trilevel place on top of your ravine is really something else. A perfect bachelor pad, with sauna, built-in stereo, the works. As the crow flies, we'd be within sight of each other, though would you believe that by the road it's a half-hour drive around the mountain? Odd, that. Anyway, if you have any objections to having me for a neighbor, feel free to say so." He paused, respond-ing to the horror in her eyes with a slowly expanding smile. "I didn't think you'd object. Here, finish this. Can you eat another sandwich?"

With the last bit of sandwich jammed in her mouth, she couldn't have talked if . . . she could have talked.

She added to the list of things she detested about Hart Manning that he had no problem talking. *Ceaseless*, that mouth of his. Once he'd finished two more sandwiches, she thought he would leave.

Instead, he started cleaning up the remains of their makeshift lunch, then poked around the dry sink until he'd figured out how it had been converted, rambling on about the import-export business he'd inherited from his family, a firm that apparently ran itself and left him free to travel around the world. Bree didn't have to do much reading between the lines. He clearly didn't care that he was presenting himself as a vagabond who lived off his family in high style, or that he had a cut-and-run philosophy where women were concerned.

Trailing helplessly after him, she stopped listening, increasingly aware that she didn't have the brawn to throw him out. As nosy as he was, he had to check every pilot light in the lean-to, examine the propane containers, fuss around the electrical box, and all the while prattle on in that sexy baritone about getting kicked out of Dartmouth way back when.

With yawns and hostile body language, she did her best to communicate boredom. Staring pointedly at the door only sent him in that direction to check the lock, frown, forage through Gram's cabinet for oil, and fix the damn thing. "I hope you had the well checked before you came here. You should have it inspected at least once a year for ground contaminants..." He glanced back to find Bree slumped in a chair in defeat, both hands cradling a chin that was wobbling with weariness.

She gave up. She didn't care. He could stay and talk until doomsday, and she was going to be the first recorded person in Ripley's to fall asleep in a straight kitchen chair.

With a strange little smile, Hart crossed to the open cupboard, set a water glass in front of her, and filled it halfway with hooch. "After you finish that, have to be on my way," he said regretfully. "I've got a dozen arrangements to make today. I can wait until you've finished every drop, though, not to worry."

He splashed a little in a glass for himself and raised

it as if to toast her. The man was mad. Bree stared first
at him and then at the unwanted liquor, then lifted the
glass and downed it all in one choking gulp. A violent
shiver of revulsion raced up and down her spine, but
he'd be surprised at what she'd do to get rid of him.

Hart chuckled. Before she could give the least thought
to what he was doing, his hands reached for hers, pulling
her to her feet. Her legs felt like Lego blocks; her spine
was trying to form an *S*. In some other world, she was
feeling several very silly reactions to the feel of his strong
brown hands on hers. It was worse when his right hand
came up to push aside the strand of hair on her cheek.

"Now, I guarantee you'll sleep without trouble this
time," he whispered. "How often do you have that nightmare, anyway?"

Her green eyes flickered up in groggy confusion; she
was unsure if she had heard him correctly. At the foot
of the loft steps, he draped both arms over her shoulders
and leaned his forehead against hers. There was a stubble
of beard on his cheeks, she noticed vaguely.

And his teeth were beautiful, straight and white. Just
a hint of curling blond hair showed beneath the open
throat of his shirt. His lips were even, top and bottom,
oddly soft, sensually parted—and she couldn't imagine
why she was standing there staring at him.

But he seemed to be standing there staring at her. The
ready smile was gone; she could feel his gaze skim possessively over the dirt streak on her cheek, the sleepiness
in her eyes, the shape of her mouth. Her flesh seemed
suddenly too hot, and too cold. And in that sudden silence, her heart was suddenly beating, beating, beating...

"I don't know what on earth you're running from,
honey," he murmured, "but life's too darn short. You
either reach out and take what you want or it's gone.
You've got to be that much stronger than the opposition

every time or they'll take advantage. Hear me?"

Vaguely. She was much more aware that he had tilted his head just slightly, that as he'd finished talking his mouth had stolen closer, that when he'd said his last word his lips were hovering over hers . . . and then taking possession.

Her breath caught in her throat at the shock of warm, smooth lips reshaping hers, molding them to fit his larger mouth. Her head tilted back, and her lashes fluttered. Something was terribly wrong. She felt engulfed, tossed in some sea; she couldn't breathe, the smell of clean, strong man and musk and brew smothered her.

It wasn't that she was affected by the kiss, because she couldn't possibly have been affected by a simple kiss, not from him. She was tired, that was all, tired and groggy and miserable, and the tiniest murmur escaped her throat when his arms slid under hers, when one of his hands suddenly pressed roughly against her spine, the other hurting her as he tugged off the rubber band in her hair.

"Sorry, honey, but that's so much better," he murmured with satisfaction. The auburn strands tumbled down to curl like silk around his fingers. His lips plunged down again. An arrogant tongue stole the moisture from her mouth, slowly probing into moist darkness he had no business probing. He was just . . . everywhere. She couldn't think. His fingers were sifting in her hair; his chest was crushing her breasts; his leg shifted forward and his arousal pressed against the lower part of her stomach—dammit, did he have to announce it?

And she seemed to have hot butter in her veins. Bree, are you even slightly aware that you're glued to a stranger? whispered a polite voice in her head.

In a minute, Bree told the small voice.

Hart's lips slowly shifted from hers, pausing to press a lingering kiss on her cheek, then on her forehead. "Off to bed," he whispered.

A few of the vertebrae in her spine managed to stiffen instantly. The word *bed* did it. Hart had a certain way of saying it, and if he thought for one minute...

He chuckled, gradually releasing her. "You know, Bree," he murmured, "I'm warning you right now—a lady who can't say no is irresistible." He sighed, touched a forefinger to her nose, and took four long strides toward the door. "I'll be back," he promised.

Chapter Four

BREE'S DIRTY FEET WOKE HER UP.

Everything else was perfect. She breathed in the perfume of blossoms and pungent woods and spring leaves. The feather bed was more giving than a sponge; its soft covering of linen nestled to her bare breasts and stomach and thighs. Birdsong disturbed the silence, but nothing else.

Except for the gritty dirt between her toes that tickled and itched and grated.

Bree's eyes blinked open. Shoving aside the starburst quilt as she turned on her back, she raised one slim leg. Filth. Absolute filth. She'd never in her life gone to bed so dirty.

One groggy eye deciphered nine o'clock on her wind-up travel clock. For a moment, she thought it must be nine at night—until she glanced out the loft's only window and saw the sunlight. She'd actually slept for seventeen hours? And without a nightmare?

Her empty stomach made an acknowledging noise, and she half smiled, leaping out of bed. Gram's hand-carved wardrobe nestled in the arch of the beamed ceiling; the cane rocker sat by the bed; and an out-of-tune spinet took up most of the rest of the space. Coming here, waking in the loft, simply felt right, as she'd known it would feel right...at least until she spotted her bedraggled traveling clothes in a heap on the floor. Next to them, where she recalled having tossed them, were brand-new jeans and camisole tops and polka-dotted underpants.

She suddenly recalled a little too quickly a little too much of the afternoon before. Her smile was transformed into a faint frown. She glanced first at the window, then to the bottom drawer of the wardrobe. Standing on tiptoe, she groped until she found a dusty key hidden in a crack between the logs above the window.

Grasping it, Bree knelt down and unlocked the wardrobe's bottom drawer. Gram's treasures were locked there, nothing anyone but Bree could have valued—old pictures, Gram's favorite apron with the bluebirds along the hem, a tarnished silver-backed brush Gramps had given her, and last—very definitely a shout of new amid the old—the telescope.

Gram had been both a bird-watcher and a stargazer. Bree had other purposes in mind. It took some finagling to twist the telescope full length, but she managed. Then, pushing the loft window open all the way, she held the scope to her right eye and squinted.

There was only one house within sight, and Gram had had a fit when it was built. She hadn't been much for concrete and man-made swimming pools and fancy skylights, and she claimed the place spoiled her view. At least the owner had had the courtesy to leave it vacant for the last few years.

Bree refocused, turning the lens. Her yard dipped low, curving down into the woods of the ravine. She could just catch a glimpse of the pond's silver water; then the woods rushed straight up through a brambly tangle of underbrush. At the top, perched as though in danger of falling, was the house built of glass and stone.

To Bree's relief, the downstairs windows were still boarded up; the upstairs ones were closed. No car sat in the carport. Perhaps Big Mouth had decided to vacation in Hawaii; at any rate, he certainly wasn't there.

Lazily, Bree yawned, suddenly more content than she had felt in weeks. There was nothing to disturb her morning. Setting down the telescope, she tugged on some clothes and vaulted downstairs. Breakfast, then a bath.

Sitting in front of a bowl of cornflakes—not her favorite breakfast—Bree kept glancing toward the door. Finally, knowing she was acting paranoid, she dropped the spoon in her full bowl, got up, jammed the extra kitchen chair against the door handle, and settled back to her breakfast.

One bowl of cereal turned into two, and then a dish of strawberries. Though she hadn't eaten a good meal in weeks, Bree was still startled to find her appetite returning.

She was the type who hadn't taken the training wheels off her bike until she was eight. She was the all-B student who never wavered, the girl who'd always been home by curfew, the coed who took computer science instead of poetry. She'd chosen Richard, a man as sensible as herself, who wanted two children, just as she did. And she'd worked for Marie as Contec's systems analyst because it was a responsible, secure job. That was Bree, a lady who made careful choices because she didn't like change or risk. She'd felt backed up against a wall for years, but she still wasn't inclined to fight her way out of the garrison.

At least that was the Bree she used to be.

The current Bree seemed to be a mess who didn't have the least idea what she was going to do next, who was eating cornflakes and strawberries as if there were no tomorrow, and who had braced a chair against the door in fear of a stranger who clearly wasn't anywhere around.

It hardly seemed much of an improvement. The old Bree had character; the new one didn't have the sense to roll up the cuffs of her pants. Tripping, Bree set down her empty cereal bowl, cuffed the jeans, cleaned up her few breakfast dishes, and grabbed a towel and soap, noting with some annoyance that Hart had purchased a brand of soap for delicate skin.

That man noticed far too much.

And she was spending entirely too much time thinking about him. After a quick brush of her hair, Bree left the cabin, padding barefoot through the tall, mossy grass. Woodpeckers were going crazy in the hickory just outside; they always did in spring. She felt like humming as she pushed aside branches and overgrown brush on the old familiar path through the woods.

The woods were virgin. The trees stretched easily four stories tall, their trunks three times bigger around than she was. Sunlight had to sneak through the umbrella of fresh spring leaves overhead. Logs had fallen over the years; rhododendron chased over them and kept on going; patches of white trillium had crept over the old path; and pockets of bluebells were scattered wherever morning sunshine fell.

With the towel slung over her shoulder and her hands jammed casually in her pockets, Bree lifted her face to the warmth of an Appalachian morning and felt lighter than she had in weeks. A rabbit bounded in front of her and out of sight; she caught the white fluff of a deer's tail from the corner of her eye.

From the crest of the hill, she had her first glimpse of the triangular pond, not so big you couldn't swim across it, not so small a rowboat wouldn't have ample room to explore. Memories flooded back to her . . . Gram teaching her to swim, Gram's wrinkled old skin all goose bumps as she laughed, tossing shampoo to a younger Bree, Gram showing her how to impale the wriggling worm on her fishing hook.

The mirror of blue was mountain fed and never much warmer than melted snow. Sun-bleached stones formed the shoreline, and Bree sauntered to the water's edge, dipped a toe in, shivered, grinned, and froze as her fingers were halfway to the waistband of her jeans.

She wasn't alone. Her lungs suddenly rationed all air going in, and then she quickly ducked behind a pair of ancient pines and crouched down. There was no mistaking that golden mane, even soaking wet.

Damn the man. Even if he'd managed to rent the house, he didn't need to have discovered the pond. *Her* pond, for that matter. And if he *had* rented the place, where was his car? And why on earth hadn't he opened a window if he'd slept up there?

About to take a fast hike back to her cabin, Bree hesitated. Hart's head had just popped up from the water, his scalp seal-slick, his face ruddy from the bracing chill. He dipped back under, his arms soundlessly slicing through the water. As he raced the length of the pond, his body skimmed just below the water's surface.

Disgusted, she realized he was stark naked. And that the tan on his face matched the tan on his rear end. At the far shore, he slipped underwater again. Seconds passed, and Bree suddenly frowned. More seconds, more . . . Fear gripped Bree's heart. She vaulted to her feet at the same time that he finally surfaced, and she crouched on her haunches again, feeling like a fool.

The next time she looked, he was standing in waist-deep water, facing his side of the ravine. Water was sluicing off his golden shoulders, glistening on sun-baked flesh. Noisily splashing into the water, he started a lazy backstroke, his kick obscuring most of Bree's view, but she caught a glimpse of the riot of curling wet hair on his chest, silver in the sun. How she hated excessive hair on a man.

When it came down to that, everything about him was excessive—shoulders, hair, limbs, even the expansive way he moved, as though overfilled with energy . . . *male* energy. Excessive hormones, Bree diagnosed dryly, ignoring the little voice in her head that reminded her she could certainly leave if she was so annoyed.

And she *was* going to leave.

Soon.

Hart went down and under again, staying beneath the water at least a minute, but this time she wasn't foolish enough to panic. He was not drowning. He obviously knew what he was doing in the water—the devil did deserve his due—but when he surged up only fifty feet from her, her breath most unwillingly caught.

She wasn't susceptible, but some women would undoubtedly find him a faultless specimen. A caveman should have those shoulders, and the way he carelessly dragged a hand through his hair ... well. He really was an example of primitive virility. No big deal—that kind of man had never turned her on—but being such a sludge of a human being, he deserved at least that lone brownie point. It was only fair.

Bree had always been fair.

And she was now slightly confused as to how he'd managed to have her clinging to him like ivy the afternoon before. The hooch? Exhaustion? Another screw loose?

She'd put the kiss out of her mind in the same way she ignored creaks in the night; maybe they scared you for a minute, but you knew you were really safe and forgot them. The longer she watched Hart, though, the more a restless curiosity wandered through her mind. What kind of lover would he be? Masterful and all that nonsense? A reasonably small woman could get crushed under all that ...

Bree.

Shape *up.*

Nudging a knuckled fist under her chin, she sighed. When he was gone, she would take her bath.

He was underwater again. She frowned, her eyes scanning the small triangular lake. Before she could blink twice, he'd surged up not twenty-five feet from her, facing the spot where she was hiding in her cover of trees.

"Seen enough, honey?"

Bree froze.

Hart threw back his head and laughed. "Curiosity killed the cat, they say. If that's your problem, you'd better be darn sure you've got all nine lives intact." In chest-deep water, he took a step closer, and then another.

Four steps later the water only reached his knees. Bree scrambled to her feet. The man had *no* shame. *None.* And how the devil could the man be aroused in water that was only one degree warmer than melted snow?

"Hiding behind trees at your age," he chided. "An honest-to-God voyeur would have chosen much better cover. Or dyed that mane of red hair. The T-shirt fits . . . delectably, I see. You've even got a little life in your eyes this morning. No nightmares last night? Talking yet?"

No, she wasn't talking. She was *stalking*. Back home. *Alone*.

Red hair, was it? Now, those were fighting words. And never mind the matching red on her face.

Sunbeams sent down dusty rays on the old oak counters of the general store. "Looks like you're going to try out a few of your gram's old recipes, Bree." Claire studied every item before putting it into Bree's sack. "Could have knocked me over with a feather when I saw you coming in here. Thought that cabin was going to stay empty for sure."

Claire rubbed the tip of her nose, eyeing Bree's smile with a curious look. "Barker over at the pharmacy, now, he mentioned that you'd gotten a little uppity since you were here last. I told him that was nonsense. I knew you as long as I knew your gram; ain't no way you ever had your nose up in the air . . . and who's to say you got to talk to everybody, anyway? That's forty-seven ninety-six, sweetie. What's wrong, darlin'?"

Everything. Small towns, for openers. And three hours

of failing to communicate, of being misunderstood, and of giving old acquaintances the wrong impression—an impression that she'd suddenly become standoffish. She felt as if her head was about to come off.

Bree counted out the money, looked at Claire, and abruptly swung her purse onto the old wooden counter. "Claire," she scribbled, "I have laryngitis. I'm not being unfriendly. I *can't* talk."

She shoved the note across the counter along with her money. Claire read the note aloud, flicked her eyebrows up, and beamed at Bree. "You poor thing. I told Barker you hadn't turned into no snob." She leaned on the counter, ignoring the two people behind Bree who were expecting to get waited on. "I tell you what my pa used to do for a case of throat trouble. Don't go to Doc Felders, now— he don't know nothin'. You take a spoonful of common tar, three spoonfuls of honey, the yolk of three eggs, and a half-pint of brew. Beat it good with a knife, not a spoon, bottle it up, and dose yourself good a few times a day. You'll have that throat fixed up in no time."

Bree nodded her thanks. If she'd had a voice, she wasn't sure she would have been capable of a verbal thank-you for that particular advice.

"If you want me to, I'll make some up for you and bring it over..."

Bree, grabbing her grocery bags, quickly shook her head.

"Wouldn't be no trouble at all..."

The real problem with lying was the endless trouble the little fibs could get her into. It took twenty more minutes before Bree was free to sidle through the door with her arms aching from the weight of her grocery bags.

The car had been preheated under a South Carolina midafternoon sun. There was barely room for Bree—the back seat, the floor, and the passenger seat were crammed with parcels. She'd known after the first fifteen minutes in town that this was going to be her one and only trip for a while—unless those temperamental vocal chords of hers decided to function again.

The main street of Mapleville was dusty and quiet. The post office was brick, but the old flour mill and general store and pharmacy were frame buildings that hadn't seen fresh paint in a decade or two. Bree had always loved the sleepy, lazy town, and the people in it as well, but heading home was a relief. Patience, Dr. Willming had counseled her.

She was fresh out of the commodity. She'd hurt several people's feelings that morning by not responding to their friendly questions. She'd earned a good headache simply by traveling a few miles and being unable to communicate. And a man she thoroughly detested had walked all over her while she just kept taking it like some helpless ninny. Bree was *not* helpless, and she was damned tired of *feeling* helpless.

Hot and miserable, she carried sack after sack into the cabin. Gradually, as she unpacked her purchases, she began to feel better. If the three hours of shopping had been grueling emotionally, she *had* found everything she needed to keep her busy for the next few weeks. Buying groceries had been a nuisance, but the rest of her purchases were sheer luxuries, memories of things she'd once loved to do. Gram had taught her to use the old spinning wheel, and she'd bought two sacks of wool from the old mountain man up the rise who raised sheep. She'd also purchased dye to color the wool once it was spun. And baking—on the *immediate* agenda was fussing with Gram's old recipe for Rich Bride Cake, and for days after that she had equally delectable plans. Her sacks were full of wheat flour and rye flour and yeast, ground rice, mace and nutmeg and currants; ginger and molasses and hops—things that few cooks used anymore.

And the old witch from the north of town—well, she claimed she was a witch—had yielded cedria and bergamot and vitriolic acid and citronella, some of the old-fashioned ingredients needed for making perfume. Gram had taught Bree the craft as a child, and as she grew older Bree started to create her own scents—better than those of the professionals, according to Gram. That, of course, was silly, just as silly as her frivolous childhood dream of making perfumes as a career. But for these few weeks, she was free to be just as silly and impractical as she pleased, to do only the things she really loved doing. She might even have time to get one brew of scent going before she started baking.

If she weren't so hot. Thank heaven Claire had managed to come up with a bathing suit from the far back of the store. The style of the suit had almost made Bree laugh, but at least until her luggage arrived she could get clean in the pond without risking exposure to any loudly vocal exhibitionists.

When she had put away all her purchases, Bree squeezed some fresh lemons for lemonade, downed two glasses of the refreshing drink, and tapped a bare toe in the silent room. Hot sunlight poured through the windowpanes, peaceful and cheery, yet she couldn't seem to settle into doing anything.

The heat must be causing this nagging restlessness. The night would cool up fine, but right now her jeans were sticking to her legs and her hair was curling damply around her temples. Popping up to the loft, she peeled off the stiff denims and camisole and dug out the bathing suit she'd just put away.

She put it on and grimaced at herself in the cracked old mirror in the corner. The suit was a one-piece black number with a little skirt, high necked with thick straps, the kind that had gone out of style several decades ago. The general store didn't exactly stock the height of fashion. Furthermore, the built-in bra seemed to be made of whalebone. It was cool, Bree reminded herself, and that was all she'd wanted at the time, something that was

cool and concealing. No one was around to care or see
... Her eyes flickered abruptly to the telescope still lying
by the window.

Gram had spent hours with that telescope, looking for
whitecrowned sparrows and ruby-throated humming-
birds. Bree adjusted the lens, quickly scanned the trees
for Gram's old favorites, and zoomed in ... accidentally
on the house at the top of the hill.

He'd taken the boards off the windows, she noticed.
The yard had been mowed, not an easy task on that steep
rise. A chaise lounge now stood on the patio that jutted
out over the ravine. And there was someone in the upstairs window, rubbing a cloth on the dusty panes ...

Bree abruptly lowered the telescope, readjusted the
lens, and held it to her eye again. Not *someone*. A woman.
In a shocking-pink confection that a brazen hussy might
have the nerve to call a bathing suit.

It *certainly* hadn't taken him long to get established
in the neighborhood.

Actually, that model of housekeeper looked imported.

She blinked again, squinting harder into the lens. Good
Lord, there were two of them. The second came with
tiger stripes. And that *child* didn't know enough to buy
a suit that fit her.

Bree lowered the telescope, and grabbed a towel.

Downstairs, she picked up a bottle of shampoo and
headed for the door. Her suit, she thought wryly, was
hardly necessary. She was going to get her skinny-dipping
bath in freedom after all. He'd found someone else to
play with. More than enough to keep him busy.

A little bath, a couple hours of sunbathing, then her
projects ... *Safe* echoed through Bree in one huge, dis-
gruntled yawn.

At the pond, she abandoned the bathing suit and flung
it toward the nearest bush. The sun caressed her bare
skin as she walked with head thrown back to the shoreline. She waded knee deep into the icy water, then thigh

deep, then arched into a shallow racing dive.

Water rushed around her limbs like icy silk. She flipped over and began a lazy backstroke, swimming the length of the pond once, and then again. Her senses seemed to burst into life, senses that had been dormant for weeks now. She was conscious of everything—the heat of sun and the chill of water, the whispered softness of trees and woods, the look of her own white skin under clear water, the feel of her hair sensuously streaming around her face when she slipped underwater.

In time, she stretched her limbs to the sun like a sensual kitten and then waded to shore for her shampoo. As she wandered back to waist-deep water, she spilled a little of the soft liquid into her palm and soon had a mound of sweet-smelling lather in her hair. Such luxuriousness felt delightful. A dollop of white foam fell between her breasts and trickled down; she arched her breasts for the sun and kneaded the shampoo into her hair and felt utterly, deliciously, wantonly wicked.

Richard would have been appalled to see her standing naked in the woods. So, come to think of it, would her parents. And anyone else she knew. Bree was not a brazen, sensual lady and never had been. She was just... Bree. All her life she had been just... Bree.

Maybe the shampoo bottle held a secret formula for washing away dissatisfaction, because at the moment she exulted in playing mermaid. When she dived to rinse off, her hair streamed behind her, and she played a few minutes more, although her flesh was starting to feel cold. A half-hour later, shivering, she shook the water from her skin as she waded back to shore. Bending to pick up the towel, she straightened, loving the warmth of sunlight on her bare skin.

Almost against her will, she found her eyes darting around, seeking out shadows in the woods, absently scanning the densely covered rise to the top of the hill... Abruptly, her hands stopped patting her skin with the towel as if she were putting on a strip show. Then her spine straightened into a more natural posture, and she stopped whipping back her hair like a forties movie star.

Dammit, Bree. You've been freezing for at least a half-hour, and you may as well quit acting like a damn fool. He's not there. You knew that even before you came down here.

The softly caressing towel turned into a rubbing punishment. Would you get that damn man out of your mind?

Chapter Five

AT ELEVEN, Bree collapsed on the feather bed, tested her little finger to see if it had the energy to wiggle, discovered it didn't, and contentedly closed her eyes. This once, she knew she would sleep. The day couldn't have been fuller, with shopping and swimming and a quick experiment with scents and an entire evening of baking. And in the peace and silence of the woods, she was certain her nightmares were behind her.

But the dream came back in the darkest hours. Always, it was slightly different. New details would hauntingly tug at her memory: the way the clouds had hung in charcoal-gray shadows, the face of someone in the crowd, the song she'd been humming as she left Gram to get the car.

Always, the end was the same. She'd let herself be talked into taking a frail old woman outside on a frigid day—her fault. They'd shopped for hours—her fault. She'd left Gram alone—her fault. She'd wasted a few minutes bringing the car around, the exact minutes during which the purse snatcher had attacked Gram—her fault. She was the one who had let it all happen. Wrong choices . . . all her fault.

And the siren kept screaming in the dream. The night pressed down on her; sheets writhed around her like chains. She had loved Gram so much, and the siren kept screaming, along with a silent scream that no one else ever heard.

"Bree. Stop that caterwauling and get your little butt down here so we can both get some sleep."

Bree's eyes flew open. Disoriented in the darkness, she glimpsed the illuminated hands of the clock next to her. 2:13. Vaguely, she was aware that her heart was pounding, her forehead damp, that the sheet was twisted around her.

"You hear me? If you don't come down, I'm coming up."

The voice was a low, lazy baritone, delivering the threat in bored tones. In fact, she heard the yawn that followed it.

Hart. Unmistakably.

Heart still thundering, Bree frantically untwisted the sheet and groped for a robe. There wasn't one. Naturally. She hadn't anticipated needing a robe *or* a nightgown; she'd gone to bed naked because the night had been hot. There was certainly no reason not to, when she was positive she had bolted both doors.

"Bree."

She tripped on the quilt, trying to reach the wardrobe in the dark.

"Honey. You really shouldn't try my patience at two in the morning. At the count of ten, I'm coming up."

Her fingers frantically touched cotton, polyester, linen, silk, and finally the quilted fabric of her robe, grabbing it from its hanger. Hurriedly wrapping the short garment around her, she rushed barefoot to the loft stairs, groggily aware of a dim, flickering light below.

She took one step down, and two more—enough to be able to bend over and look, blinking hard. The tears were already dried on her cheeks, forgotten; and if her body was still trembling slightly, she put it down to rage.

"Now, let's not panic. I put on my pants, see? Nothing to get nervous about. Get down here," he ordered irritably.

Nothing to get nervous about? A double sleeping bag

was spread out on the floor by the wood stove. Two
candles were flickering in tin lanterns. The Rich Bride
Cake she'd spent the evening making was still on the
kitchen table—but had a distinct and massive dent in it.
And an almost naked man was glowering at her from the
bottom of the wooden steps—and never mind his jeans.

Hart's massive chest was bare, his shoulders the color
of hot gold by candlelight, his chest sprayed liberally
with silvery curling hairs. His hair was tousled, his cheeks
dark with stubble, and his midnight eyes glinted at her
like wet blue stones. The civilized veneer was gone; he
could have been a mountain man, as primitive and amoral
and rough as any of the hermits who stalked the back
hills carrying their shotguns.

"Honey, *don't* climb down a flight of stairs in a robe
that short for anyone else, would you?"

He lowered his head. She scrambled down several
more steps, even though she never for a minute believed
he could see what he was claiming to see. "What the
devil do you think you're doing here? How did you get
in?" The questions tried to tumble from her lips, but
though her mouth moved, she had no voice at all.

For a moment, there was no sound at all in the cabin.
Hart just looked at her, his eyes rambling with deviltry
over her wildly curling hair, the faint dampness on her
cheeks, the vulnerable pallor of her face by candlelight.
Bree flushed, for no reason, tucking the robe closer around
her in a protective gesture that produced a desultory smile
from Hart.

"Unfortunately, I finished the hooch when I came in.
I checked around—thought you'd at least have a beer
in the fridge, but no. Not even wine. God save us from
teetotalers," Hart said disgustedly. "I can hardly believe
we're stuck with milk."

He disappeared through the open door of the lean-to,
and Bree let out an impossibly huge sigh, combing her
fingers hurriedly through her hair. He was such an ex-

asperating man . . . yet in some murky corner of her head, she wasn't totally miserable about his being here. The ache in her heart lessened, the post-nightmare trembling had stopped . . . every time Hart was around she was too busy being furious to feel depressed.

"You left your window screens unlocked. Doesn't do much good to bolt all the doors when a bear could push a paw through the screen and get in." He returned from the lean-to and thrust a glass of milk in her hand. A lazy grin split his face; that teasing smile below intensely dark eyes still seared on hers from above. "Now, don't throw it, honey—not that I'd really mind. Milk may be a bitch to clean up, but I'll take that look in your eyes any day over the way you looked a few minutes ago. So you had another little nightmare, did you? More alligators under the bed? I would have been here last night if I hadn't had so damn much to take care of. Just sit down, and we'll have a little talk."

She jabbed a furious forefinger at the sleeping bag.

He nodded. "You didn't really think I was going to leave you alone here to scream your heart out all by yourself? Besides, it was hot up at my place."

A blatant lie. His house had central air conditioning, and her nightmares were her business. Bree's lips tightened as she motioned even more angrily to her cake.

"Terrific stuff. It was still warm when I came in; I could smell it when I was ten feet from the door. Now, I know I took a little piece, but that was hardly my fault. You shouldn't bake like that if you don't want it eaten. Incidently, you've got quite a contraption there." He motioned to the "bubbler" she had set up in the corner by the dry sink, where she'd played with a formula for perfume hours before.

"I had such high hopes when I first walked in here that you were making a little moonshine; it *is* a still, isn't it? But that smell isn't remotely related to liquor. In fact," Hart drawled lazily, "the scent has distinctly aphrodisiac qualities. One of the first things I noticed about you on the plane was that scent you wear—nothing heavy, is it, honey, just whatever it takes to drive a man over the edge. Are you a witch in secret, Bree? Woops. I forgot the lady isn't inclined to talk back."

Hart twisted around, spotted her purse on the floor by the dry sink, and bent over, rummaging around in it until he withdrew her notepad and pen. "Drink your milk," he ordered. "And then—just this one time—we'll do a little communicating your way. Against my better judgment. One way or another I'd like at least a *hint* as to why you get the screaming meemies at two in the morning. Unless you've got something better to talk about?"

He motioned her to the sleeping bag, as if he expected her to sit there. Bree stood rooted to her spot in the shadow of the stairs, one hand holding her robe closed and the other clutching the cold, sweating glass of milk.

"Ah. We get the feeling the lady doesn't want to talk about it. Well, fine, Bree." Hart sprawled in a kitchen chair and raised one bare foot to the opposite one with a lazy yawn. "I told you before that it's terrific finding a woman who doesn't constantly prattle on and on, demanding constant attention, interrupting my every sentence..." He yawned again, a flashy grin zipping across his face. In that crazy, flickering candlelight, he looked like a demented tawny bear.

"Believe me, honey, I can talk for two. You want to hear about the time I drove a car into a swimming pool? That's a good story. It happened to be the principal's car—in the suburb of Los Angeles where I grew up—and the principal's daughter happened to be in it. Happened to be in the car, that is, not just the suburb. Problems sort of compounded on that one, since I was only fifteen and didn't have a license—"

My God, he could *talk*. On and on...Bree stood motionless in the corner. She took a token sip of the milk, but never considered sitting down. Even to perch on the steps was tantamount to giving him permission to stay. And Bree couldn't do that.

Tension crackled around the room like a resounding echo. It had nothing to do with Bree's nightmare. It had nothing do do with Hart's naturally lazy baritone, soughing on and on about a dozen irresponsible escapades he'd had in his youth. The tension was strictly sexual; it rippled disturbingly whenever her eyes met Hart's—and his never once left her face.

"So they let me take over the business. Uncle Harvey was sick of the constant travel; Dad was still trying hard to believe I could turn into an upstanding human being if given a little responsibility." Hart yawned and paused long enough to lift both feet onto the kitchen table, crossing his ankles. "Lord, you have beautiful eyes. Sometimes soft as water, sometimes full of fire..." He raked a lazy hand through his hair, staring at her. "Anyway, easiest way to make money I've ever seen. Don't know why the hell I went to college—except maybe for the pleasure of getting kicked out, like I told you. All I really needed to make good was a peddler's mentality, a little larceny in my character, the ability to butter a few palms ... Getting a little tired, honey, or are you just swaying on your feet because you like music?"

Vaguely, it occurred to Bree that there was something sneaky about Hart. For one thing, he was always yawning when his eyes were most alert. He worked so hard to present his character as totally irredeemable, when no one could have packed all the irresponsible, selfish actions he claimed he had into one short life. He insulted her often, but suddenly he would say something kind ... and he *was* here, and he'd gone to a lot of trouble to find a house close to her...

Maybe it was his personal hobby, driving women crazy.

He was good at it. Her bare feet had grown roots. She'd stood still for the better part of an hour and just let him rant on, and cobwebs must have collected in her brain, because she knew darn well she'd been staring at him for most of that time. Nightmares faded when Hart was around—it was a trick he had. A terrible trick, that blue-eyed stare that held hers in a jail-like lock, as though he wouldn't let her go, wouldn't let her mind wander to any subject but him.

"Well..." The kitchen chair tipped down; Hart's feet dropped to the floor. "I think it's time we both got some sleep, anyway. This time I think we'll insure against nightmares, though. Do you want to sleep down here with me, or shall I take my sleeping bag upstairs?"

Her jaw sagged, just slightly.

Hart bent over and pushed one of his two pillows toward Bree, clearly making room for her on his double sleeping bag. "If the mosquitoes weren't so bad, I'd suggest the porch, but without repellent or netting, this is probably the coolest place we can find. Snuff that second candle?"

He opened the tin lantern over the dry sink to blow out the first candle. The second one was on the table. Bree, rubbing one arm absently with the cold fingers of her other hand, didn't move. His arrogant assumption that they were sleeping in the same room surpassed even his usual audacity, but she wasn't certain how she'd fare in a fistfight.

His eyes leveled on hers over the flame of candle on the table. "Don't be too foolish, Bree," he said in a low voice. "We both know I'm not leaving. And that you're not afraid of me." He snuffed out the second candle himself.

In the sudden total blackness, she heard him shucking off his jeans, then lying down on the sleeping bag, then ... silence. A lonely, frightening silence. All silences had been frightening to Bree for these last weeks.

One of her bare feet shifted forward, then the other. Moonlight bathed her profile in white mist for one moment before she crouched down, fingers blindly reaching for the spare pillow and quilted surface.

"Here."

He tossed a cotton blanket over her, most impersonally. Tugging it to her chin, Bree felt . . . ashamed of herself. If it had come to a fistfight, she knew darn well she would have won by forfeit. Hart was without morals or character, but she just knew he wouldn't lay a hand on an unwilling woman . . . There was no pretending she'd been forced, coerced, or browbeaten into lying next to him.

Minutes ticked by. Her eyes gradually dilated until she could make out hazy, moonlit shapes and shadows. Lying on her side at the edge of the sleeping bag, she was conscious of her own tense, weary limbs. The cabin still smelled like fresh-baked cake, like the elusive flowery scent she'd made earlier, like wood and the sweet odor of the vanilla candle just snuffed, like . . . man.

Like Hart.

No sane woman would trust him. Like an abrasive, Hart had scratched the serenity she'd expected to find here—but she didn't want him to go . . . not just yet. She wasn't ready to face the darkness alone again—the night, the dreams, the terrible, vulnerable feeling of loneliness.

Gram's spirit was in the cabin, as she'd known it would be. And by day, Bree was feeling an increasingly strong belief that she hadn't been crazy to burn her bridges, to chuck her job, her fiancé, everything that was familiar. She'd made some wrong decisions in her life; all she needed was the courage to turn herself around. But by night, fears eroded that brand-new, so fragile courage. In her heart, she couldn't rid herself of her guilt, of her conviction that Gram had died because of *her* wrong choices.

And whether it was crazy or not, she wanted, very badly, to be held.

A massive sigh echoed next to her, and she stiffened. "Nothing like sleeping next to barbed wire to relax a man. Not tired yet, honey?"

Hart propped himself up on one elbow, gently pushing her shoulder down until she was lying flat on her back. A huge, shaggy head leaned over her, so close his wet, dark eyes were only inches away, so close the male smell of him surrounded her. "Want to know a very good cure for insomnia?"

Bree shook her head. She was crazy, not stupid.

"Honey's the cure," he murmured. "A spoonful at a time. You thought I meant making love, didn't you, Bree? Put your hands on my shoulders," he whispered.

She shook her head again, alarmed.

"Now, Bree." He might have been scolding a recalcitrant child. He lifted one of her limp arms and locked it around his neck, then the other. With one smooth motion, he pushed aside the cotton blanket and lay down on his side, cocooning Bree in his arms.

There was a great deal wrong with lying length to length against a man you didn't like. And worse than that, he felt exactly as Bree had been afraid he was going to feel—warm and big and infinitely safe. Bombs didn't move Hart—how on earth could anything harm her with him in the way? Like the stroke of a velvet feather, his palms slid down her shoulders to the small of her back, moved back up to gently push her cheek to the hollow of his shoulder, then back down again.

He stroked . . . and he stroked. Arms loosely around his neck, face buried against embarrassment in the warm flesh of his shoulder, Bree closed her eyes and just . . . let it be. Her robe was tangled between them; vaguely she was relieved that he at least wore briefs; a little voice in her head kept trying to convince her there was something wrong here . . . but nothing felt wrong. If the sexual vibrations were powerful, her need to be held was infi-

nitely more powerful. Snuggled close to Hart, she felt
irrationally certain that she could take care of herself
tomorrow if he would just handle the night.

"Bree."

Her eyes fluttered open.

Hart cleared his throat. "I don't know if this is doing
something good for your insomnia, honey, but it's sure
wreaking havoc with mine."

Instantly, she tried to back away from him. Just as
instantly, his arms tightened around her. "I didn't say I
didn't *like* it," he growled. "Stay where you are."

She stayed, very still. For a minute or so. There seemed
to be a perverse demon in her head, though, because
after a minute passed she shifted her cheek, just a little.
Enough so that her smooth, warm lips suddenly lay against
the hollow of Hart's throat, and rested there.

Hart growled again. This time the sound rumbled from
deep within his chest cavity. "Don't tell me the woman's
decided to come out of hiding?"

So amused, as he leaned over her, brushing his lips
in her hair, rubbing his cheek on her smooth, soft skin.
Bree felt, as usual, half inclined to kill him. Maybe she
was having a tiny problem with cowardice about her
choices right now; maybe there were some decisions she
just couldn't face yet. But to accuse her of *hiding*—that
just wasn't fair.

And if he thought she was attracted to him, he was
crazy. She was curious, that was all. Surely any woman
who'd been quiet, morally upstanding, and sensible all
her life had a secret wish to be ravished, just a little, by
an unprincipled, good-looking rogue who knew too much
about women?

And Hart did have a gift for making the nightmares
go away. *Dammit*. His mouth dragged a slow chain of
kisses down her throat, down toward the V of her robe.
A foglike cotton clouded her brain; her flesh seemed to

be raising goose bumps all over; her heart was becoming utterly confused, pumping in double time.

There was too much of him. Everywhere. He moved with the lethal slowness of a mountain cougar, his lips prowling her vulnerable spots... behind her ear, down again to her throat, whispering dangerously around the quilted robe that just covered her breasts. Through a tumble of fabric, she was well aware that his leg had sneaked between hers, that his palm was making lackadaisical curls down her spine to her bottom, that he was rubbing her deliberately against him.

And she was rubbing back.

"That's it, honey. Tell me what you like," he whispered. "God, you're responsive. I knew the minute I met you..."

Only Hart would mistake simple curiosity for intense sexual responsiveness. Totally against her will, her fingers climbed his bare shoulders, traced the knotted cords in his neck, skimmed into the thick, rumpled mat of blond hair. Her eyes closed, the lids far too heavy to stay open. His mouth found hers in the darkness and molded itself to her lips, parting them.

Her neck arched back and her limbs turned liquid. It was a very foolish sensation, like feeling caught in the rain naked, like feeling drenched in liquid softness. Hart's tongue swirled inside her mouth, playing games with her tongue. Between them, her robe twisted open, helped no small amount by his hands. She tensed.

"You have beautiful breasts, Bree... ssh. Let me see."

He raised himself up just a little, very gently pushing aside her robe. She seemed to be trembling, for no reason whatsoever. It was the moonlight coming in. The soft silver bared her flesh, illuminated the shadow between her breasts, made the orbs look white and swollen. His finger traced the shape of one, around, beneath, making a circle, and then a smaller circle, and then just softly touching the peaked tip. A whispered murmur escaped her throat.

His eyes lifted to hers, all blue-black liquid. "Do you know what I want to do, honey?"

She shook her head.

"I want to kiss them, Bree. I'd like to bury my face between your breasts; I'd like to wash those little red tips with my tongue until you cry out. I want to feel the weight of them in my hands; I'd like to feel them crushed against me..." He bent down, to press a butterfly kiss ...on her throat.

Below, the heartbeat between her breasts was going like a time bomb, as if to say, what about me? You just promised...

Hart slowly lifted his head again. "But you're going to have to tell me what *you* want, Bree. Do it, honey. Tell me. Tell me, Bree..."

Instinctively, she parted her lips...but there was no sound. No sound at all. He just looked at her, waiting, and the moonlight washed over her bare breasts like a shower of heat.

"You have to tell me," he whispered again. "You want me to make love to you, Bree?"

Yes. It was crazy and it was wrong...and she'd never wanted anything more. Her body was sending out a frantic *yes;* he could hardly have missed the message.

Abruptly, he draped the robe over her again. "When I was younger," he murmured, "I used to enjoy the role of seducer. The hunt and chase and all that nonsense. It *is* fun, honey, but not nearly as good as when two people come together with honesty, both knowing what they want and willing to admit it." He pressed one last kiss on her forehead before rolling over on his side. "I think you know what you want, Bree. But you're going to have to tell me when you're ready."

Bree stared at his broad back, a little stunned to be so abruptly deserted. So he'd suddenly turned virtuous?

And the lecture he should have taped.

Less than five minutes later, he was asleep.

Less than five hours later, Bree woke up alone. She knew there was no one next to her even before she opened her eyes; the warmth and the smell of him were gone, the weight of his arm around her waist . . . Bemused at the sudden flood of memories, her eyes blinked open, to lazy ribbons of sun pouring through the cabin window.

Groggily, she stood up, shaking her head to clear the cobwebs. That didn't really work, nor did splashing cold water on her face. Folding up Hart's sleeping bag and blanket, she felt another sleepy rush of images invade her mind. Hart had pulled back, yes, and he'd done it in his usual insensitive way, trying to goad her into talking . . . as if she had a choice. She wasn't forgiving him that, but there were other pictures floating in her head. As she dropped his sleeping bag on the front porch, she remembered the woman who'd deliberately awakened the sleeping bear, who'd willingly lain next to him. She remembered an abandoned response that had come from nowhere . . . a response that started with Hart, with some crazy thing he did to her when he touched her. Free. She'd felt free. To touch, to entice, to just . . . let go. To be a very different kind of woman than she'd always thought she was.

Put on your clothes, she reminded herself vaguely. Back to reality, Bree. He's a selfish, arrogant man; it isn't wise to forget that. You just ditched a perfectly decent fiancé; your life's a mess; and he's the last man on earth you would want to get seriously involved with.

All true. That didn't shake the bemused mood, the ridiculous feeling that she was utterly beautiful this morning. Silly. As she climbed the steps to the loft, the sun already felt hot, but she didn't realize what time it was until she flicked an eye on the bedside clock. Eight. She'd really only had five hours' sleep. A small smile touched her lips. She'd come to this cabin for rest, but she'd had very little since Hart came into her life.

Pulling open the wardrobe, she grabbed a camisole top and jeans. By sheerest chance, her eyes settled on the telescope. It was supposed to go in the bottom drawer, not on the floor of the wardrobe, and enroute to putting it away properly she lifted it to the window.

There was action at the top of the ravine. The bare cement patio was about to be crowded with lawn furniture. A single chaise longue was already there. So was Hart, wielding one end of a white wrought-iron table. A little brunette was wielding the other end, laughing, dressed in a pair of indecently short shorts and an open-necked blouse.

From a distance, the brunette had kind of a cantaloupe for a face, but that was primarily because Bree hadn't focused the telescope. And wasn't going to focus it. She felt as though someone had just socked her in the stomach. Jamming the telescope in the bottom drawer, she tugged on clothes and thumped barefoot down the stairs with a furious scowl.

Call me when you evolve, she thought crisply as she flung bowl and cornflakes on the kitchen table. Darwin was wrong. Men were the lowest species, not the highest. *Snakes* went into heat less often than Hart Manning did.

She ate her breakfast so fast she got hiccups. Water splashed every which way as she attacked the bowl with suds and dishcloth, hiccuping on every second breath. By the time she'd cleaned up the suds sticking to the floor and herself, her nerves were sandpaper. He'd deliberately made her believe that she could mean something to him. He'd deliberately touched her with tenderness, seduced her with those lazy eyes of his.

She found herself staring at the white bowl, sparkling clean now twice over, and scowled again. In one quick movement, she sent it winging toward the door. It smashed obligingly. So did another plate. Actually, so did two cups and a saucer.

Silence followed. The sun beamed in sunnily on the white shards of porcelain. Bree's hiccups were gone. And she was so sick of silence she could have screamed.

Chapter Six

WITH THE SUN blinding her, Bree stared grimly at the rusty latch on Gram's old shed. It just didn't want to give—she'd been trying for the better part of an hour. She tugged again at the knob, then finally threw her weight against the door to force it open. With an eerie creak, the door swung in, Bree pitching forward with it. In that sudden dank darkness, her shin immediately connected with something bulky and hard. Her skin dented; the old tool didn't.

Using her entire vocabulary of four-letter words— silently—Bree massaged her aching shin and waited for her eyes to adjust to the darkness.

The last five days just hadn't been her best. Her luggage had arrived, but so had letters from home. Her mom wanted her to return; she was worried about her, and Bree hated being the source of that worry.

The letter from her ex-boss had disturbed her even more. Marie was blithely ignoring her resignation and lining up projects for Bree to tackle "as soon as you're feeling better"; Contec "is seriously hurting without you." Bree's first impulse was guilt for leaving Marie in the lurch; her second was wariness as she reminded herself that Marie was an expert at using guilt to manipulate people; and her third was a feeling of being totally unsettled, a state of mind that still hadn't left her.

In the meantime, she'd had to buy an entire set of

dishes, since she seemed to have shattered all the old ones. And her sleep had been constantly interrupted by her own personal night watchman, Hart Manning. Sleep? There was little point in even trying.

Squinting into the dark corners of the old shed, Bree stepped over an old wooden crate and sighed. The front yard needed mowing. Unfortunately, most of Gram's tools seemed to have disappeared. A pitchfork was accumulating rust in the corner. Her eyes skimmed over Gram's old gardening gloves, a small spade, a hand saw, an ancient scythe . . . but there was nothing remotely resembling a lawn mower or even clippers.

With hands on hips, Bree shook her head. The scythe would have to do, dull and awkward though it was. It looked like something that belonged on a Soviet flag, but its original purpose a century ago must have been to cut grass. You could always go home, Bree, said a little voice in her head. What exactly are you accomplishing by staying here—you haven't had any rest; you're still not talking. You're worrying your parents; and at least you had a safe, secure job . . .

Gingerly lifting the scythe from its hook, Bree took it outside and wielded it awkwardly in the sunlight with a stubborn cast to her chin. *No*. Not yet. For herself, she might still be confused over what she wanted to do with her life, but for Gram . . . She felt in some indefinable way that she owed Gram something—something that she could pay back only by being here.

But Hart was making it extremely difficult for her to keep her mind on what she owed Gram. He'd showed up every night, once at ten, another time just before eleven, another at precisely ten forty-three. Each time he spread out his sleeping bag downstairs, made an unholy racket settling down, and disappeared before Bree awoke the next morning.

She hadn't acknowledged that he was there. She'd lain upstairs in Gram's sensuously soft feather bed, stared at the moon, and twiddled her thumbs, fuming. She'd spent hours during the day thinking of what she was going to say to him . . . when she got her speech back. And she'd spent the hours at night worrying that she would fall asleep and have another nightmare, that Hart would come up to her, that she would behave . . . foolishly again.

Sooner or later, she'd fallen asleep those nights. There'd been no nightmares, but he was driving her nuts. Or maybe she was driving herself nuts, knowing she wasn't doing a damn thing about him. She'd seemed to spend her entire life letting things happen to her, letting other people direct her actions; it had to stop. The big stuff takes care of itself if you handle the little things first, Gram used to say.

The yard certainly filled the little-things slot. The grass was knee high and straggly. If the project seemed woefully minuscule compared with the momentous decisions facing her, at least she wasn't moping around the cabin like an exhausted zombie. Enough was enough.

Bree swung the awkward scythe, by the grace of God saved her left leg on the back swing, and noted without surprise that the blade hadn't severed so much as a blade of grass. Whipping back her hair, she determinedly tried again.

The blade was not exactly in the best shape in terms of sharpness. The sun beat down in a fever of heat; flies buzzed; Bree's madras shirt and short shorts stuck to her; and blisters formed on her right hand before twenty minutes had passed.

Three hours later, Bree collapsed flat on her back on the front porch of the cabin. She had just enough energy left to turn her head and survey the demolished lawn. Even, it wasn't. Short, it was. The blisters on her palm were killing her; her throat was so parched she would have sold herself from a street corner for a glass of water; every muscle felt cracked like old leather . . . and she was grinning like a fool. She'd done it. *Thought you couldn't handle it, didn't you, Bree?*

Yawning, Bree closed her eyes. In a moment, she would get up. She so desperately wanted a drink; her palm needed first aid; she longed for a bath and change of clothes. To heck with all that, she was so tired she could sleep like a baby.

"*Exactly* where I was afraid I'd find you. Trying to nap in the middle of the day. It's no wonder you're not sleeping nights."

Bree didn't jump. Familiarity breeds contempt, as they say. If she hadn't actually *seen* him in several days, Hart had still managed to interrupt every single occasion when she'd tried to get any rest. Besides, her heart instantly recognized him by pumping in and out like a windy bagpipe, even before she opened one eye—Hart not being worth opening two for.

As it happened, he was worth less than one. Gone was the urbane sex symbol in Italian suits. He wore his derelict straw hat sideways, his cutoffs showed hairy legs, and he hadn't bothered with a shirt, just a fishing pole.

His eyes were dawdling over her long legs in the short shorts. "Come on, lazy lady. Leading the life of Riley, it's no wonder you can't sleep nights. If so many complications hadn't cropped up at my place, I'd have been over here before to keep you busy during the day. Like now. Did I mention we're going fishing? And I see your clothes arrived. No bras in your suitcases?"

If that crack was supposed to bring a rise, it didn't. And as far as Bree could tell via telescope, Hart couldn't have too many problems at his place. His harem did all the chores.

When she didn't move, Hart tch-tched. "The bait's worms. You probably can't handle that, but I figure you could at least row the boat. Talking yet?"

Why were all her new dishes put away, when she

needed them to throw at this moment?

"You want help getting up, or do you think you can manage that all by yourself?" Hart shielded his eyes with a closed palm, his dark blue eyes peering down at her. "Honey, you have a button that's undone," he said politely.

Bree's eyes whipped open, her fingers groping for the front of her blouse as Hart lazily surveyed her front lawn. "You *did* do a little something today, I see," he drawled. "I *thought* you'd get off your duff sooner or later—couldn't just sit around and do nothing forever, now, could you? I'm not a big advocate of industriousness, but when it becomes too much of an effort even to open your mouth, I draw the line."

Bree sat up furiously, ready to hurl back a slightly blue retort—in mime—but Hart had already turned away. His eyes narrowed on the scythe resting against the cabin wall.

"You didn't use *that* to cut the lawn?" His head whipped back to her, his dark eyes no longer lazy but suddenly blazing with anger. "You damn fool, you could have killed yourself! The thing's half as big as you are. Did you ever once think to *ask* someone for a little help? What the *hell* do you think I'm within shouting distance for, anyway?" He added in a low growl, "Let me see your hands."

She'd show him her hands the next time she had the inclination to dance naked in the village square. He advanced a step; she retreated, bottom first and chin up, into the shadow of the cabin porch. Unfortunately, bottom first and chin up were not conducive to speed.

The next thing she knew, Hart had snatched her wrists and turned up her palms for inspection. "I'm going to kill you," he announced darkly, "as soon as we wash these and put some antiseptic on them. Go ahead. Give me an argument, Bree."

Bree struggled valiantly for patience. Some men

couldn't help being insufferably patronizing. On the other hand . . . He didn't move for an instant. It was seconds, not minutes, before he pulled her to her feet and propelled her inside to the sink. But in those seconds Hart's face was inches from hers.

His cheeks were red with rage. He hadn't shaved, his lion's mane was crushed beneath his hat . . . and his touch was infinitely gentle on her hands. A lover couldn't have touched with more tenderness. She found herself staring, mesmerized.

It was becoming an effort to keep hating him, in spite of his harem on the hill. The man had a magic quality, the ability to fill her world when he was around, blocking out everything else. He was worse than a sliver—worse than a *bad* sliver. He got under her skin and stayed there, saying aloud things she'd been thinking herself: that she'd been lazy, that she couldn't talk because she'd been running away from life, that it was about time she *did* something about herself. Really, he was a very cruel man. She ached for Gram and she was confused; everyone wasn't a bulldozer like Hart . . . but he made her feel that those were only excuses. In her heart, she agreed with him.

She didn't *like* the man. She just felt . . . attracted to him, like a bee to honey, like a magnet to metal. Maybe she was just experiencing a bad case of loneliness? Regardless, this was definitely the first chance she'd had to get back at him for his patronizing bossiness, the only *real* reason she trailed after the ranting bear, toting two fishing poles while he carried the open can of worms. As they approached the pond, she saw a canoe, tugged up on the stone beach and outfitted with a tackle box and two pillows.

Fishing, was it? A tiny smile of triumph hovered on Bree's lips, but she masked it when Hart turned to her. "You get in first, lightweight," he ordered. "And don't get all prissy about baiting the hook. I'll do it for you."

So kind. Bree stepped into the freezing water with bare feet, and lifted her leg carefully over the side of the canoe.

"Put the pillow behind your back," he ordered. "And leave the paddles alone, with those hands. I'll handle that."

Orders, orders, orders. Bree leaned back against the boat cushion, crossed her legs, and savored the warmth of dappled sunlight on her cheeks as she anticipated the comeuppance she knew was awaiting Hart. She'd watch him fish, all right. The pond was fed from melting snows on the mountaintops; a thin stream of a silver waterfall constantly kept it filled. Fish, however, did not spontaneously appear just because there was water. There were *tons* of places to fish in the area, but this was not one of them—unless Hart had stocked the pond in the last few minutes.

"Now . . ." He shoved off, lifted a dripping leg inside the canoe, and settled lazily, facing her. After he got them out to the middle of the pond, he lifted the dripping paddle inside and just let the canoe sway to and fro in the breeze. He reached for one of the fishing poles and frowned at her. "You're going to get your nose all sunburned."

Before she could stop him, he'd flipped open a tube of white cream and dabbed a streak of it on her nose, nearly tipping over the canoe in the process. "Better," he said with satisfaction. "There are sunglasses in the tackle box if you want them."

Attaching a worm to his hook, he cast his line in the water, stuffed a pillow behind his back, pulled his hat down, and did a reasonable job of looking as if he were taking a nap. Which was exactly the kind of fishing Bree suspected Hart knew how to do, being such a self-proclaimed expert at laziness.

Determinedly, she reached for the other pole. He *wasn't* sleeping, or he wouldn't have suddenly tipped back his

hat in time to grin at her as she reached for the worm
with her mouth all screwed up as if she'd just eaten an
unripe persimmon. Gram had never baited Bree's hook
for her; Bree was certainly capable of doing it herself,
but that didn't necessarily mean that she had ever liked
worms.

Having nothing better to do, and certainly wanting to
sucker Hart along on this "fishing" expedition of his,
Bree expertly cast her line and snuck a glance at Hart
... who appeared to be napping again. He missed her
move—a cast five thousand times better than his own.
It hardly mattered, since there weren't any fish, but it
was a point of pride. She was sick to bits of his constant
accusations that she failed to *do* anything, as if she were
an incompetent little ninny.

While he napped, she cast and recast, slowly reeling
in her line, whirling it around her head to toss it into the
water again, her hook landing *exactly* where she aimed
it. The fool might just learn something, if he'd open his
eyes. Only when she made an unobtrusive attempt to rub
off the gob of white cream on her nose did she realize
he was awake.

"I wouldn't," he said mildly. "You know I'll just put
more on. We can't have you broiled like a lobster, lazy
one." Hart sighed, throwing one leg over the gunwale
of the canoe. "This is the life, I swear. Sun, surf, and a
silent woman. What more could any man ask for?"

Bree might have asked for a little less ego on the part
of her companion. Weren't his little darlings on the hill
enough for him? A silent woman, indeed. He obviously
loved it when she took his verbal bait, so she refused to
show by even a flicker of expression that he was getting
to her. Setting down the pole, she leaned back against
the cushion and...

Relaxed. Dammit, she *was* relaxed. She knew darn
well she looked bedraggled in the wrinkled madras blouse
and old shorts. Her hair hadn't been brushed in hours;

she wasn't wearing a bit of makeup . . . but somehow all of the tension of the morning was stealing away, replaced by a somnolent sense of well-being. The steady slip-slop of the boat, the sun's warm, soothing rays, even Hart's own laziness seemed to be infecting her. A few days ago at the airport she'd felt so terribly *raw,* inside and out. It occurred to her how rarely she didn't feel *on,* even for her family and friends, playing roles and fulfilling expectations. But with Hart . . . well. For someone who'd already seen you at your worst, you hardly felt obligated to put on airs.

Trailing her good hand in the water, Bree threw back her head and felt the sun beat down like a healing balm. She wasn't exactly attracted to him, she thought idly. It was more fascination. Any woman would undoubtedly feel *some* of that fascination.

It was those midnight-blue eyes, for one thing. The phrase *bedroom eyes* was such a cliché; still, if she were ever inclined to take a man to bed because of a pair of eyes, those were the pair. The way his lips parted in a lazy, unbearably sexy smile; the sheer blasted mischief he wore for an expression half the time. The touch of his hands, the tender way he kissed, the manner in which his mouth and body moved in an embrace, pulling her in like an intimate undertow, making her forget rhyme and reason and . . .

Hurriedly, Bree mentally catalogued Hart's safer physical attributes. Hairy legs, and Lord, they *were* hairy. Big feet. Bony knees. The shoulders of a mastodon. The silliest cowlick in the center of his head . . .

He suddenly lurched forward, pushing his hat back from his forehead, grinning at her. "You're relaxed, Bree, aren't you?"

She nodded warily. Why did that sound like a trick question?

"I knew you would be, if I got you out on the water. I thought to myself, She's smarter than that; she's lived

here before and will know damn well there aren't any
fish in the pond—but when I saw you casting, I knew
we were home free. When you think about it, *someone*
has to buy encyclopedias from the door-to-door sales-
men. Now, don't get upset. That wasn't meant as an
insult. It's an absolute delight to find a woman who'll
follow a man's lead in this day and age . . ."

Hart sighed. Bree parted her lips to let out a detailed
torrent of abuse . . . and when her vocal cords refused to
respond, something inside her snapped. Mindlessly, she
threw her weight forward, and the canoe precariously
tipped.

"Easy—" Hart yelled.

Easy *nothing*. Frustration boiled up like a witch's cal-
dron inside her; she'd give a fortune for a working tongue.
Unthinkingly, she leaped to her feet, saw Hart's hands
grab wildly for her, felt the canoe lurch violently . . .

And the next thing she knew, she was over her head
in the water. *Icy* water. She surged to the surface, batting
furiously at her curtain of soaking hair, and swirled around
until she spotted the canoe. Treading water and gasping,
she took one look at Hart—who was leaning back against
his cushion, roaring his head off—and determinedly swam
toward the canoe.

"Now, Bree . . . It *was* funny. Where's your sense of
humor?"

She pushed. And pushed. The canoe rocked wildly in
the water, but refused to capsize.

"It won't work, sweetheart. You know how canoes
are made. Easy to tip from the inside—good heavens,
didn't you know that?—but not that easy to overturn
from the outside. Oh, shoot," he said mildly. "I seem to
have made you angry again."

Abruptly, Hart dropped his crooked grin. In the middle
of the sunlit pond, his eyes held hers, blue and fiercely
compelling. "And you are angry, aren't you, honey? Yell.
Go ahead. Scream at me, Bree. Don't you want to tell

me what you think of me, sweetheart?" he whispered like a teasing taunt. "Come *on*, Bree."

She sent a furious wave splashing in his face, and then whirled around, starting a rapid crawl toward shore. She heard him sputtering for an instant. Not nearly long enough.

"Don't you want to fish anymore?" He called after her, almost managing to sound disappointed. "Never mind, I'll see you tonight. I've got a dinner date, but I'll be there around nine. Lay out my sleeping bag for me?" He added in a roar, "And put some more antiseptic on your hand!"

By seven, Bree was alternately fussing with tiny glass bottles and eyedroppers at the kitchen table and worriedly glancing at the clock. Normally, she could count on work with her perfumes to get her mind off anything, but this evening she was having trouble concentrating. The balsam and citronella were already in; so were the drops of civet and orange oil. Flipping the stopper from the vial of bergamot, she squeezed the eyedropper and started counting. *Four, five, six . . .*

Her eyes flipped up to the clock again. Are you really just going to let him come in here and walk all over you again? What are you, a doormat?

Fourteen, fifteen, sixteen . . .

Locked doors hadn't worked. But then, locked doors were kind of like locked tongues—excuses for inaction. She'd always had good excuses for letting other people direct the flow of her life. Gram would have been . . . disgusted with her.

Twenty-nine, thirty. Pushing the stopper back into the vial, she reached for the heated wine. Once she had poured the proper amount of special alcohol into the mixture, she glanced again at the clock, bit her lip, and started slowly stirring the fragrant liquid.

Hart . . . bothered her. It was more than his irritating

attitude and pushiness. It was *him*. The man. When he
was around, she always felt close to losing control, and
Bree never lost control. He'd accused her of anger, and
he was right. But anger at herself or at him? It was him,
of course. It *had* to be that she was just continually angry
at him.

She carried her perfume concoction into the corner
where she'd set up the tiny still. It would take days before
either of the new perfumes was ready, but the cabin was
already filled with the blended soft scents of fruits and
flowers. As Bree put away the last of her ingredients,
she glanced at the clock again. Eight-thirty, and if he
was actually going to arrive by nine . . .

He was *not* going to find a doormat. Tossing the towel
on the table, Bree bolted for the loft steps and took them
two at a time. Within ten minutes, she'd burrowed into
Gram's wardrobe and stripped off her jeans. After
changing clothes, she made a trip to the old shed, and
after that she dragged the old rocker out onto the porch.

By nine, she was waiting for Hart. Dusk had settled
around her like a gentle mist; the birds had stopped sing-
ing, and animals were sneaking from the woods for a
peek into the clearing. Bree's bare feet were stuffed into
a ragged old pair of men's boots. Her calico skirt was
gathered at the waist and reached midcalf; above it she
wore a drawstring peasant blouse. A straw hat perched
on her head. She was the image of a mountain woman,
and Bree hadn't forgotten the pitchfork on her lap. Maybe
she couldn't talk, but then, they say actions speak louder
than words. Hart should be able to figure out the general
message.

Her chair creaked violently as she rocked, until she
found herself yawning. Nine passed, and then nine-fifteen.
Flanking her were two citronella candles, ostensibly to
chase off the mosquitoes but actually for light—that way
she couldn't possibly miss his approach, even if his car
made no sound.

His car made plenty of sound, roaring through the quiet night like a restless lion on the prowl. Instantly, Bree stiffened, laid the pitchfork across her lap just so, and kept on rocking, her eyes narrowed as the car came to a halt fifty feet from her.

When Hart stepped out, her rocker started a furious creaking pace. This wasn't the lazy Hart of the pond but the polished Hart of the plane. His hair was carelessly brushed back, catching the silver of moonlight, and his shoulders looked mammoth in a cream linen suit—one of those Italian tailored jobs of his. If he'd had a carnation in his lapel, he could have gone to a gangster's wedding; as it was, he passed for damned gorgeous . . . and just a wee bit on the formal side, given the wilderness behind him and the occasional cry of a lone cougar.

"Bree?"

With her booted toe, she nudged his rolled-up sleeping bag down the porch steps as he slammed the door of his car. The pitchfork remained at the ready. He hadn't been dining with any mountain boys, not in that attire. The woman had undoubtedly been breathtaking, and if even for a *second* he thought he was coming here for a free dessert . . .

"Bree?"

She rocked, her chin cocked at a stubborn angle. Hart stalked forward, his jacket open and one hand loosely in his trouser pocket . . . at least until his eyes finally adjusted to the candlelight and he caught a good look at her. His expression went blank, but she could feel his assessment, from the tacky straw hat down to the boots. His eyes rested for long seconds on the pitchfork—and being Hart, he had to spend some time scouting out the territory inside the peasant blouse. A poor choice, she should have thought of that.

Still, she figured she'd done a fairly good job of getting her message across . . . particularly when for a few moments one could have heard a pin drop. Hart just stared with those eyes as dark as the woods behind them, no expression on his shadowed face that she could read.

And then he slumped back, drawing a hand over his face. A shudder racked his body. Bree scowled. Another shudder, and suddenly his ridiculous guffaws were filling the night. He stumbled back. He said something, but he was so choked up with laughter she couldn't make out his words.

With no respect for his suit whatsoever, he collapsed on the grass with his head bent over his knees, laughing in absolutely uproarious humor.

Bree leaped up and hurled the pitchfork off to one side. Funny, was it? She ran down the steps so fast she nearly tripped, her hands on her hips and her hat gone flying. "You ... *varmint*. You ..."

The croaking voice seemed to be coming from miles away. Bree was too incensed to care. The hoarse whisper cracked and stuttered and creaked like a rusty record, but it gradually gained momentum. "You *skunk!* You egotistical, domineering, patronizing, know-it-all, interfering, insensitive, overbearing, pushy, sneaky ..."

The litany just kept coming.

Chapter Seven

STILL SEATED ON THE GROUND, Hart wiped the tears of laughter from his eyes. Leaning back on his elbows, his mouth twisted in a lopsided grin as Bree hovered menacingly over him. "Honey, you're talking!"

She was so mad she was shaking, words tumbling out like spilled rusty nails. "How many women do you have up there anyway? Thousands? If you think you're camping out here again tonight, you'd just better not count those chickens, Manning. You wouldn't be welcome here if I were a ninety-year-old virgin. I'll sleep in the same room with you again when hell freezes over. You wouldn't know a *moral* if you were painted with them. You—"

"Keep it up," Hart encouraged. "You're doing terrific, Bree." He leaped to his feet, grinning hugely. Upright, he let out one more exultant whoop of laughter and started stalking toward her. "Honey, you're *talking!*"

Bree was not to be diverted. "You wouldn't know a principle if it shot you between the eyes. You have the sensitivity of an ox. Insensitive? Dammit, you've been *cruel*. You're cruel and you're pigheaded—"

"You did it, honey! You finally did it!" With another bellow of laughter, Hart tugged off his jacket, balled it up as if it weren't the most luxurious Italian linen Bree had ever seen, and hurled it at the moon.

She lost a little of her momentum, having completely run out of breath and being slightly stunned to see his

expensive jacket decorating a bush at the edge of the
woods. When she glanced back to him, her eyes narrowed warily and she folded her arms protectively across
her chest. He was advancing very slowly, with a devilish
grin that boded trouble for her sanity. She backed up a
step. And then another. "Hart. I don't know what you're
thinking, but *don't*."

"*You*, lady, owe me a thank-you."

"*A thank-you!*" she sputtered incredulously. "All
you've done since I've met you is interfere and order me
around and act like a patronizing, chauvinistic—"

"Hey. You're talking, aren't you?"

Actually, she was still retreating, until the back of her
skirt rubbed against the porch step. Her tormentor continued to stalk. She put out her hands in a gesture pleading
for mercy that would have made a hardened criminal turn
chivalrous. Hart kept coming. "Now just *listen*—"

He raised his arms, clearly with every intention of
snatching her. She ducked before he could and, grabbed
her skirts so she wouldn't trip, darted out of his reach
and down the porch steps. She lost a boot in the process.
Feeling like a perfect fool, she raced across the grass
and promptly lost the other boot. She had more speed
barefoot, but when she glanced over her shoulder, Hart
was gaining on her. "Listen. We're two grown people,
for heaven's sake. You be*have*—"

"*You* stand still."

Maybe when it snowed in June. Bree ducked and
circled and dodged, moonlight streaming through her hair
and her heart pounding. Hart might be a powerhouse,
but she was faster. The chase sent an exhilarating high
through her blood; she felt as if she'd just showered in
champagne. It was so silly, so childish . . .

And when Hart snaked an arm around her waist from
behind, she collapsed on the grass—not because he'd
used any force, but because she couldn't continue to run,
she was laughing so hard.

They lay sprawled within feet of each other on Bree's
haphazardly mowed grass. Hart's chest was heaving as
hard as hers was; his roars of exultant laughter filled the
night. His husky chuckles were catching—worse than
chicken pox, Bree thought wildly, but he was so crazy,
and she felt such deep, endless relief that her speech had
returned, and the night was sultry and warm, with no
one around—

And she was totally unprepared when Hart's hands
sneaked across and grabbed her. One minute she was flat
on the grass, and the next she was sprawled in an ungainly
mass on Hart's belly.

The sudden midnight gleam in his eyes filled her vision, and then cool, smooth lips rubbed at first gently
on hers, then settled in like a famished man for a Christmas feast.

Bree made a muffled, startled sound. Hart ignored it.
Silence suddenly vibrated through the night. Then in the
distance, an owl hooted and the wind restlessly whispered
through the new green leaves, but there was really just
Hart, the sound of his uneven breathing. The sound of
hers.

A dozen things made it difficult for her to regain her
common sense. The grass, for instance. The sweet smell
of grass and earth surrounded her. And other things also
interfered with her mental functioning. Hart's breath
smelled like peppermint—she could taste it. She could
taste the whispers in the woods. Really, she could. And
her hair was all tangled in Hart's hands, curling around
his fingers, and her eyelids were suddenly too heavy to
stay open. And his mouth . . . his mouth was the real
reason she couldn't move. His lips were slanted over
hers, greedily sapping her common sense, making tender,
wooing, teasing promises . . .

All blood drained to her toes and was replaced by
warm whipped cream.

"So sweet, Bree . . . so sweet." Shards of moonlight

gleamed in Hart's eyes as he tilted his head back. He just looked at her.

Only the way he looked at her made her skin flush. And her skin was already so hot she was plenty flushed. "Listen," she said vaguely.

"Not just this minute, honey." He bent to place a row of kisses, a very neatly aligned row, from the tip of her ear, down the vulnerable cord of her throat. Along the neckline of the peasant blouse. One finger slipped the blouse off her shoulder. His other hand was sliding up the calico skirt, from calf, to knee, to thigh, to...

"Hart."

"Busy," he murmured.

An understatement. Bree's fingers tangled in his hair when his chin nudged the peasant blouse on the swell of her breast. She sucked in a shallow breath. Hart... knew what he was doing.

A rush of sheer hot-blooded lust cascaded through her bloodstream. Lust was just the kind of feeling that Bree had always avoided. Lust was sort of an animalistic craving; it was depraved, immoral, don't-care-about-tomorrow, wicked.

Exactly the way she felt. Good old responsible Bree was deserting ship, and the waters were very deep, very dark, lusciously inviting. It was really all Hart's fault. By rights he should have been a selfish, take-her-quick kind of lover. Instead, he was clearly trying to make her believe he'd never encountered a breast before.

He traced with a fingertip. He explored with his lips. Then his tongue. He fitted the orb in his hand; he rubbed the tip with his thumb; he took the tip in his mouth and sucked and lapped until—for absolutely no good reason, except that she'd never considered doing it before—she ducked her head and softly bit him on the neck.

Hart chuckled. "You like it just a little bit rough, Bree?"

Before she could breathe, he'd wrapped his arms

around her and they were rolling, over and over, down the slope of the spongy lawn. Grass caressed her back, then caressed his. Moonlight played in her eyes, then his. Even as they tumbled, his lips claimed hers with a fierce, sweet pressure; their legs tangled and for seconds at a time she felt the intimate weight of him, the power of him, the man of him.

She breathed in that scent of danger, but there was no time. Roughly, swiftly, his hands were possessively traveling over spine and bottom and thighs; her heart was racing, racing . . . A shocking little tap on her bottom was followed by a soothing circular rub of apology. Breathless, they suddenly rolled to a stop. Bree was on top of him, her breasts crushed against his white shirt. She was breathless and dizzy and as on fire as she could ever remember.

And Hart's eyes were open, a half-smile on his lips. "And sometimes do you like it just a little bit soft, Bree?"

He pressed a kiss on her forehead, as soft as a butterfly and slower than a languid awakening from sleep on a winter's day. Two more kisses settled on her eyelids, closing them effectively. Hart shifted, cradling her as he turned her on her side, his lips moving in slow motion, tenderly teasing, savoring. Very gently, he claimed her hand and coaxed it down to his thigh. Very gently, his palm glided over her stomach and ribs, pausing to cover and knead a breast, treating the swollen flesh as though it were infinitely fragile, infinitely precious. Very gently he kissed her nose, her lips, her hair, and traveled down to the nape of her neck. Her heart pounded, not gently at all.

"Tell me," he murmured gruffly. "Tell me, Bree."

She buried her face in the column of his neck, pressing kiss after kiss in the open throat of his shirt as she un- buttoned it. Her fingers were awkward, trembling still from the intimate contact with his hard manhood, sheathed not very effectively in his suit pants. Rock would have been softer. And the thought of him inside her sent shivers of anticipation up her spine.

Maybe she was stark raving out of her mind. But if she was . . . it had to be with Hart. No one else. Not like this. Ever, ever, ever . . .

"Tell me," he repeated.

She felt as if he were depriving her of life, when he shifted back from her and stood up. With a small smile, he tugged at her hands and drew her up in front of him. Not the wisest of moves. Her legs were Silly Putty. And her leaning up against him didn't make removing her blouse any easier for him. Seconds later, the delicate fabric lay in a soft white puddle on the grass. Warm night air whispered over her bare skin. Hart dipped down to taste her moonlight-bathed shoulders. And neck. And throat. She tossed her head back restlessly.

"Now, Bree."

"I can't."

"You can."

"It isn't rational," she said desperately, her eyes raised to his. "You want me to pretend there haven't been moments when I . . ." Her voice broke. "I'm not sure I like you, Hart."

"Honey." There was patience in his tone, but his voice was strained, and husky to the point of hoarseness. "You've got . . . *maybe* . . . ten seconds to tell me what you want."

"I . . ."

"You want me to walk away, Bree?"

He would; she could hear it in his voice. And Bree knew exactly what he wanted to hear. She'd sent him all the yeses in body language; it wasn't enough. Hart just wasn't the type to settle for stainless when he could have sterling.

Really, he was despicable.

"Yes," she whispered.

"Can't hear you."

"Yes," she whispered more clearly.

"Can't hear you."

"Hart, I want you!" she yelled irritably. "Do I have to shout it from the rooftops?"

Hart leaned back and offered her a very quick, very wicked grin. "Yes," he whispered.

An instant later, he swung her up into his strong arms; his lips stayed crushed on hers as he carried her across the yard to the porch. The citronella candles flickered; she remembered that later. She remembered the look of Hart as he shed his clothes, as he fetched the sleeping bag from the grass where she'd thrown it earlier. She remembered the terrible attack of trembling she had when he finally stole all of her clothes. It wasn't . . . that simple. She'd never played around.

You'd think he knew.

He was flame to her fluttering moth. He tempted her with the light, with the warmth, with the fire, never pressing. It was her choice, to mold herself closer to him. Her choice to touch him, to open for him, to invite him intimately inside her, to risk the aching fear that he would take her high but no higher. It was Hart's choice to make intimacy natural between them, to ensure that she didn't come back from the skies until she was exhausted, and sated, and flushed, and damp all over, and . . . so exhilaratingly well loved that there were tears in her eyes.

The two candles flickered in the darkness. Beyond their corner of the porch, there was another world, ominously black, filled with leaf rustlings and shadows and the occasional shine of small eyes in the woods. On the porch, wrapped up in Hart's arms with the sleeping bag for a mattress, bare as a baby and utterly safe, lay Bree, her cheek resting on his shoulder.

Hart wasn't sleeping, but his eyes were closed. Bree kept stealing glances up at him. His chest hair was a wiry blond mat, circling his navel and stretching up over his heart. His shoulders were golden; strong ribs, flat stomach . . . his thighs were muscular, and when the composite was put together, the label was man. A very powerfully built man, and even an exceptionally handsome man, but still just . . . man.

There was nothing to explain why that specific body next to her had turned her into a wanton, wild creature of the senses, capable of intense, uninhibited pleasure. Or why she felt comfortable with him now, when she knew darn well she should be reading herself a riot act of guilt, reproaches, shame, and disgust.

Thoughts whirling in her head, she spread a hand on his chest and watched the long blond strands of hair curl around her fingers. "Hart."

"Hmmm."

"I don't want an affair."

His lips brushed her forehead. "Your voice is still coming out a little rusty, but it's sexy as all hell. Or is it always that way?"

She cleared her throat deliberately. Hart chuckled. "I mean it," she said firmly.

He shifted to his side, nuzzling his lips sleepily around the shell of her ear, letting one hand run lazily down the length of her. "You know, I was beginning to worry about you. On the nontalking business. I figured maybe when you ran out of plates to throw, you'd have to come through with a little verbal exchange, but you were so stubborn . . ."

"*Stubborn?* I only *came* here because I was supposed to get heaps of rest and recuperation—"

"Who said?"

"After five million doctors said . . . don't, Hart."

"What do *they* know?" Paying no attention to her batting hand, he leaned over to run his tongue over the raspberry tip of her breast. He watched as the nipple responsively hardened and tightened before his dark eyes traveled back up to hers. "They know nothing that matters about you, honey. Nothing."

She sucked in a little extra oxygen, her lungs seeming to need it. "You're not listening," she accused him.

"Sure I am."

"I don't just . . . race into relationships. And I certainly don't—"

"Sleep around?" he supplied.

For two cents, she would have wiped the small smile off his lips with a scrub brush. Instead, she buried her head in his shoulder and closed her eyes. "It's not as if you don't have plenty of options besides me," she said dryly, thinking of the harem she'd seen through her telescope. Not to mention whomever he'd worn the cream linen suit to dinner for.

"That sounds reminiscent of 'pick on someone your own size,'" he said gravely. "Or else it's a subtle inquiry as to how involved I am with other women at the moment. Honesty's easier, Bree, but I'll try to read your mind. I went to dinner with an old man named Reninger, a friend of my father from way back. He's about four feet eleven, seventy-three if a day, and couldn't conceivably turn me on in a bikini. I had a gift for him, some jade carvings. That should settle your doubts about this evening, but if you want a catalog of the women I've slept with over the years—"

"You know, I may kill you yet. Every time you open your mouth, I feel the general urge. That's part of the problem. You don't sleep with people you want to murder."

"Is that a new American proverb? Maybe a potential slogan for a bumper sticker?"

"How do you want to go? Boiled in oil? Voodoo? A simple drowning?"

"Such talk. And I haven't yet heard my thank-you for getting you to talk."

"I beg your pardon. If you think you deserve an ounce

of credit for that, when all you've done since I've met you is *push* and *patronize* and—"

"And it all worked. I want my thank-you." He leaned over her. The pads of his thumbs caressed her cheeks; the weight of his chest crushed her breasts. He planted one heavy thigh between hers, pinning her beneath him. "I think," he murmured, "I want you now, Bree. One of Manning's oldest maxims: Never hesitate even a minute to go after what you want in life. And there is no question how much I want you. There hasn't been from the moment I laid eyes on you."

His mouth pounced . . . but slowly. Bree's hands fluttered aimlessly for a minute or two, and then she gave in, her hands climbing up his arms to his shoulders, holding on. Hart was an unpredictable carnival ride. She had the terrible feeling it was useless to ask to get off halfway around.

Even worse, she knew she didn't really want to get off. One more round of insanity, Bree . . .

"You're going to have to open your eyes sooner or later, honey."

By moving an inch and a half, Bree managed to bury the rest of her head under the pillow. Until the pillow was removed. And the comforter was slowly tugged down from her shoulders to the middle of her spine to her waist. She had to open her eyes then, to grab it.

Blinding morning sunlight made her blink as she snatched the comforter away from him and tucked it around her again, glanced at the clock on her bedside table, and shook her head at Hart. "You have something against sleep, don't you? I haven't had *one* eight-hour night since I ran into you."

"But for very good reason last night, Bree. You're not having a hard time facing me this morning, are you?"

She opened her mouth, ready with a quick denial, then abruptly closed it. She wasn't having a hard time facing him. She was having a *terrible* time facing him, which was why she'd been feigning sleep for the better part of an hour.

Through shuttered lashes, she cast a frantic glance at the wardrobe, several feet away. There was no way to get from point A to point B modestly, primarily because the sheet just wasn't going to stretch that far and she wasn't wearing a stitch.

Hart wasn't either. He was standing stark naked, with one of those lazy smiles on his face . . . but it was the dark blue depths in his eyes that made her feel vulnerable. She couldn't read his expression, and she was just coming to understand that Hart wasn't at all the man he let on he was. The public Hart was a heartless, insensitive, macho-type nuisance. Now that she had her tongue back, she felt reasonably confident that she could handle that side of him. The private Hart, she was increasingly afraid, was dangerous.

He knew a lot about women, far too much about her in particular, and had a gift for making a woman feel loved—but Bree knew better.

He didn't love her, and she couldn't possibly love him. And if he'd been any kind of gentleman, he would have stolen away at dawn so she could now face alone the mountains of guilt and self-reproach for her abandoned behavior the night before. You don't sleep with a man you barely know. You don't start relationships with womanizers. You don't play with a man you're not even absolutely sure you like . . . but seem to have embarrassingly fallen in love with.

"One does get the feeling you're not used to waking up with a lover in your bed," he said mildly.

"Nonsense. I've done this hundreds of times." Making up her mind to put a good face on the lie, Bree bounced airily out of bed, her eyes staring at the wardrobe so she wouldn't have to look at him. How did other women face these mornings after the night before, anyway?

"Hundreds?"

A flush crawled up her cheeks. "Maybe thousands. As I'm sure you have." Faster than the speed of light, she dragged a thin cotton robe around her and belted it. Courageously, she faced him then, and like a coward she whipped her eyes away. To be fair, he wasn't standing there like a seductive Viking by choice; all his clothes were outside. On the lawn. Strewn. "I'm going to have to find something for you to put on," she said flatly.

He snuck up behind her while she was leaning into the wardrobe, trying to find something—*anything*—he could wear. She felt his palm on her spine like the stroke of a feather, soothing and quiet. "Bree."

"What?" she said distractedly.

"Stop being so nervous. I won't bite. There's nothing to be ashamed of. And nothing's going to happen that you don't want. Ever. Not with me."

In spite of herself, she felt the flush on her cheeks recede. Her heartbeat even pounded out a more normal rhythm. "I'll get you some breakfast," she said swiftly, and bolted for the loft steps, deciding to let him worry about what he could find to wear.

By the time he came downstairs, she'd brushed her hair and teeth, had placed two bowls at the kitchen table, and had stopped yawning every third second from a severe attack of nervousness. Hart strode right by her and went outside, returning seconds later wearing his suit pants and nothing else.

There was something terribly decadent about a man wearing five-hundred-dollar pants and no shoes. Except *decadent* wasn't the word. *Sexy* was. When he dropped to the kitchen chair and glanced up at Bree with a lazy grin, she could feel her heart plump down to her stomach, and some hot-blooded memories that she was trying to forget flooded through her. So he'd been an outstanding lover. So no one else had ever made her feel that way. So?

She plunked a spoon down in front of him.

"Are you going to let me help make breakfast?" he asked calmly.

"No help is required. You don't think you're getting anything more than cornflakes, do you?" She took a breath. "Which reminds me. I hate cornflakes; you can cart *all* of the purchases you made up to your place, and those that I've used up I'll pay you for."

"What's wrong, Bree?"

His baritone had that . . . implacable tone, misleadingly gentle and coaxing. She slipped into the chair opposite him. "Nothing's wrong."

"The lady sounds as prickly as a hedgehog, but her fingers are trembling and her eyes have the look of a wounded fawn again." Quietly he added, "Did I hurt you?"

She reached for the pitcher of milk. A drop or two spilled as she tried to pour it into her bowl of cornflakes; Hart had a napkin, waiting for her. She set down the pitcher. "Look. I just feel . . ." She hesitated. For an instant, she felt lost, staring into a pair of dark blue eyes that rested on hers as though they loved the fragile quality in her face. "I don't want you to think I'm making too much of this," she said uncomfortably. "I mean, people do this kind of thing all the time without—"

"Without what?"

"Without . . ." She motioned helplessly with her hands, having completely forgotten what she meant to say. "Anyway, last night is hardly likely to repeat itself. I really don't know what got into me—"

"I do."

She flushed to the roots of her hair. "Hart—"

"It was the most special night I can ever remember. You were beautiful, Bree. A beautiful, loving, giving, passionate woman. You've got spirit and humor, and I haven't the least idea what you've been running from— but you don't have to run from anything. You've got the strength to carry you; you just need someone to tease it out of you once in a while. And last night was not a one-night stand, so quit trying to make it sound like one."

She was staring at him, a jumble of words jammed in the back of her throat all trying to get out at once, when there was a knock on the door.

It opened. A familiar face peered in first, a woman with faintly graying auburn hair tied back in a loose bun, a soft tentative smile, and worried lines on her forehead. Behind her was another familiar face. The man was just short of six feet, with steel and charcoal hair and a slight pauch, and in addition to a wrinkled cotton shirt, he was wearing a scowl.

Bree lurched up from her chair. "Mom! Dad! What a surprise!" she said weakly.

Chapter Eight

"DARLING! You've got your voice back!" Addie Penoyer's words came out in a delighted rush, tears filling her eyes as she surged toward her daughter. "I can't believe it!"

Bree hugged her mother back, suddenly laughing. "I couldn't either. It just happened last night, or you know I would have called you, Mom."

"I don't care, as long as it *happened*. Darling, I know I should have wired you that we were coming, but I kept telling Burke that we just couldn't let you stay down here alone; we had to do something..." Addie tripped just slightly over the word *alone;* Bree turned tomato red, and behind her she heard Hart's chair scrape back.

"Look. Mom..." Bree started uncomfortably, but Addie, staring over her shoulder at Hart, wasn't wearing the maternally disapproving expression Bree expected. Maybe Hart had miraculously donned clothes in the last thirty seconds? Searching her mother's face, Bree saw Addie bite her lip slightly, glance at Bree again with joy and relief in her eyes, then gulp in a little breath. She squeezed Bree's shoulder, and then with a tentative smile offered a slim hand to Hart. "Mr...?"

"Manning. Hart, please, Mrs. Penoyer."

Bree pivoted around, startled to see Hart's normally cocky demeanor destroyed. His complexion was ashen and his movements jerky as he courteously took her mother's hand. And for some reason, he had draped a kitchen towel around his bare shoulders. The flowery pattern didn't do a thing for him. "Mrs. Penoyer." Hart cleared his throat. "I know how this must look to you, and I don't want you to think..."

Addie waved a hand in midair. "My daughter is *talking* again, Mr. Mann—Hart. If you think her father and I care about anything else—"

"Agreed," cut in an ominous tenor from the door. "Just because a man's clothes are strewn all over my daughter's backyard, I wouldn't want you to think we see any reason to be the least upset."

Another time, Bree would have been fascinated, watching Hart turn from pale ashen to dove gray. At the moment, she was too mortified. Thirty seconds of silence filled the cabin. Each one lasted about a year and a half. Nervously locking her arms under her chest, Bree turned back to her father. "Look. Dad..."

"I have every intention of marrying her, Mr. Penoyer," Hart interjected swiftly.

Bree's eyes whipped up. "Have you gone out of your mind?" she whispered. The situation was mortifying, embarrassing, and downright awful, but it certainly wasn't a death sentence.

You'd never know it to look at Hart, though. Gone was the arrogant playboy, the cocky grin. He looked awkward; actually, he looked a little silly, holding on to the towel that didn't even begin to cover his chest, anyway. And he positioned himself in front of Bree as if he intended to protect her from dragons. For heaven's sake, it was just her father.

"I don't for a minute blame you for coming to certain conclusions, Mr. Penoyer. I realize how this must look to you," Hart started gravely.

"You can bet your sweet petunias how it looks," Burke agreed.

"Dad—"

"I take full responsibility—"

"Hart."

"You're telling me something I don't know? A month ago, my daughter was engaged to another man—did she tell you that?"

"No." Hart's eyes shifted sharply to Bree's. "But it wouldn't have made any difference. She never belonged to him. I wouldn't care if she'd been engaged to forty-seven men, and I really wouldn't care if it was yesterday."

"Listen," Bree said firmly. Hart's stare was unnerving; you'd think there was suddenly no one else in the room. It was easier to whirl around in her father's direction. "Dad, if you would relax for just a minute," she began.

Burke ignored her. "My daughter," he said heatedly to Hart, "has never once in her entire life given us cause to worry about her behavior—"

"Bree was not to blame," Hart said swiftly. "I was. But just because we've only known each other a short time, sir, doesn't mean that we haven't developed feelings for each other. My intentions—"

"Oh, my God," Bree muttered at the old-fashioned word. Hart had clearly flipped out. She stepped determinedly between the two men with a frantic glance at her mother. "Look, *both* of you. I would appreciate it if you would—"

Hart very gently lifted her to one side. "Mr. Penoyer, if I could talk with you on the porch for a moment—"

"Over my dead body," Bree said flatly.

"I think that's an excellent idea," Burke told Hart, ignoring Bree, then stalked out the door; Bree tried to dart out after him but was forestalled by Hart. Actually, he came very close to shutting the door in her face . . . right after he'd tapped a forefinger to her nose in an affectionate gesture that he might have intended to be reassuring.

She could hear raised voices the minute both men

were outside, and Hart must have had his hand on the outside door handle, because she couldn't open it. Turning to her mother, she rolled her eyes heavenward. "I just don't believe this."

Addie's eyes searched her daughter's. "He's the reason you're talking again, Bree?" she asked softly.

"I . . ." Bree hesitated, glancing worriedly at the closed door. "Mom, if you'd just let me know you were coming—"

Turning to the cupboard, Addie brought out an empty mug and calmly poured herself a cup of coffee. "Darling, you don't have to tell me. I knew the minute I saw the clothes in the yard. Actually, when you didn't turn to Richard in your time of trouble, I knew that he couldn't have been the man for you. I don't know that this man is, Bree, but he must be something special to have you totally . . . change your ways."

Bree blushed.

"I'm not saying I like it," Addie added quietly, "but I am saying it's your business."

"I . . ." Bree was at a loss. Addie had always been the wringing-hands kind of mother, never the cool, calm lady she was projecting at the moment.

The door popped open behind Bree, and she whirled around. Burke walked in, and Bree's jaw gently sagged. His irate mood seemed to have vanished. His smile was typical of her father, and he'd squeezed her shoulder just like that a thousand times. "Any coffee around here?" he asked his wife jovially.

Addie was already pouring him a cup. "Bree?"

"Ah . . . in a minute." She offered her father a tentative smile, received one back, and, carefully closed the door behind her, whisked outside.

"Hart!"

He half turned from his lazy stride toward his car. He was all bare chest in the shining sun, his smile as slow as a summer morning as she reached him at a dead pant.

"What on earth did you talk to him about?"

He reached down to place a light kiss on her nose. "Football scores."

"Try another. You know darn well my dad was a little . . . out of control," Bree said delicately. Hands on hips, she felt like tapping her bare foot impatiently, but refrained.

Hart made a sweeping motion toward the yard. She glanced back, a mistake. His suit coat was spread on the grass. One of his shoes lay nearby. The other had made it to the porch. His shirt, her blouse and skirt . . . she winced. "Naturally, he was a little out of control," Hart said darkly. "If I were a father and came across a scene like that, I'd damn well kill the son of a bi—seadog."

Unaccountably, Bree's lips twitched. "Hart. Aren't you forgetting that you were the son of a . . . uh . . . seadog in this particular instance?"

"Now, don't get sassy." Hart opened his car door.

Bree's eyebrows shot up in alarm. "Wait a minute. You still didn't tell me what you said to my dad. Where are you going?"

"Home. So you can have a little time with your folks. There won't be any more fireworks, Bree, rest easy. And your father only has the weekend, which means they'll pretty much have to turn around and drive back if he's going to be at work on Monday morning. I'll be over tomorrow night around nine . . ."

"*Wait,*" Bree said impatiently. He was going too fast, Hart style. The Galahad role he'd played for her father confused her; it was out of character—the character he'd so often portrayed. Regardless, he'd interfered in her life *again,* something he had no right to do. And as for any tomorrows and specifically tomorrow nights, Bree suddenly felt as shaky as a kitten on a too-high limb.

A faint smile slashed across Hart's face as he reached for her. "Are you going to give me some nonsense about not being ready for a relationship right now, Bree?"

"Yes," she said flatly.

His fingers curled around her shoulders, his body blocking out the sun. "You know what I think, honey?"

Bree was beginning to simmer. "*No*. And I really couldn't care less—"

"I think you need someone downright wicked in your life." His lips chased her when she tried to duck her head. They homed in and crushed hers.

The problem with Hart's kisses was that he put everything he had into them. Passages from *The Joy of Sex*, ghosts of the best of kisses past, sultry reminders of the night before. His shoulders were sun-warmed, and he had this slinky way of sliding his arms around her that made her feel buried in warmth and strength and a crazy, sweet, fierce wildness. *Wicked* was the word. She felt drugged with it, long before his mouth lifted from hers, drugged with a luscious, lazy sleepiness that had no relationship whatsoever to the reality she'd always known.

Blue eyes stared down at her, as he slowly moved back. "Run from anything else you want to," he said quietly. "You'll never run from me, Bree."

And then he was gone.

Bree drove her parents through the forests of blooming rhododendron, then took them out to dinner and settled them in the loft while she curled up in the sleeping bag downstairs for the night. They talked about flowers and they talked about politics and they talked about everything that had been happening at home. But no one said a word about Hart until the following morning when her parents were having coffee just before leaving.

Her father had settled with a newspaper in the old rocker; Bree and her mother were playing with the carder and the spinning wheel. The cabin still smelled of toast and marmalade and Bree's homemade perfumes. Sunlight alternately whisked in the open doorway and disappeared; clouds were playing peekaboo with the sun.

Bree straightened from disentangling the wool fibers with the carder. "You want another cup of coffee, Dad?"

Her father rolled down his paper, suddenly staring at her. "Would you mind at least telling me how long you've known him, Bree?"

"Around two weeks." Bree poured him a cup, then perched on the stool, waiting. She'd been expecting this— was curiously relieved it had come. She'd been glad to see her parents; she loved them and cared about them, but all three of them had been oddly uneasy around one another, laughing when there was no reason, falling into a silence where there once would have been none. Bree knew the reason for that was Hart's spending the night, and perhaps, at another level, they were hurt because she'd gone against their wishes by coming here. She'd never done that before. That she'd hurt them hurt her, and guilt lanced through Bree like a toothache. She'd always tried so hard to be good to them.

"Around two weeks," Burke echoed.

Addie rose from the spinning wheel nervously. "You never did say if you liked my new dress, Bree. Last Monday I went shopping with Kathleen Romberger. You remember her, don't you? I couldn't believe the sales we ran into—"

"You really consider that an adequate time to know someone before . . . *jumping* into a relationship with him?" Burke said quietly.

With sad eyes, Bree confronted her father. "Dad, I've done nothing I'm ashamed of," she said simply. "No one took advantage of me, and no one ever will. Please accept that."

The eyes of father and daughter met, a matching clear green, more the color of sea than emeralds, more the consistency of water than stone. "You were terribly unhappy a very short time ago," Burke reminded her. "Perhaps the question I should be asking you is when you're coming home. You've got your speech back, Bree—

that's why you came here, for rest and just to be alone through that rough time. But you're yourself again. There's no reason you can't come home now."

"I'm not ready yet," she said quietly.

"Because of him."

"No." Bree shook her head. "There are some decisions I need to make. About the work I want to do, the direction I want to go now. Everything's . . . changed," she admitted haltingly.

"Because of a man you've only known a very short time," Burke insisted quietly.

"Burke, I really think we should be packing up," Addie intervened swiftly. "You know we've got almost a six-hour drive ahead of us . . ."

She rambled on for a minute or two. Bree, shoving her hands in her pockets, leaned back against the wall, her eyes never leaving her father's face. When her mother had finished talking, she spoke in a quiet voice. *"Yes,* I've only known him a short time, but he's got nothing to do with the changes I want to make, Dad. I took a wrong turn in the road; it's that simple, and Gram's death made me see it."

"Bree, don't talk about it," Addie admonished worriedly.

Bree touched her mother's shoulder reassuringly. "I'm not about to lose my voice again," she said gently. "But as far as Hart goes, Dad, he's not the reason I'm staying here."

Burke hesitated. "I just don't want to see you hurt, sweetheart. I've thought a lot about what Manning said to me, and he made his feelings more than clear where you were concerned. But it wouldn't matter how good a man he is, if he isn't what *you* want and need." Burke scratched the back of his neck, the way he always did when he was nervous. "You know, it was a devil of a lot easier being a parent when you were of grounding age. You're grown, Bree. I respect you as an adult, and

I respect your choices. But as your father, I know you're at a time in your life when you're vulnerable. He's a good-looking man . . ."

Bree shook her head. "Since when have I ever been swayed by a pretty face?" she said teasingly.

"Bree—"

"Look, Dad. I know what your first impressions were, but you'd like him if you gave him half a chance. Hart's the kind of man who does what he thinks is right no matter what other people think. He makes me laugh, and he makes me *think*. And there's something there I never had with Richard. Also, he . . . takes care of people, and he does it in such a way that you never even realize that's what he's doing, and . . ."

"Burke, I really feel we should start packing," Addie interjected, her eyes darting from father to daughter.

"Yes." Burke's eyes searched his daughter's face as he rose from the rocker. He smiled suddenly.

The smile didn't register with Bree. She was busy gnawing at her lip, startled to hear herself defend Hart. Defend Hart? Heck, her dad hadn't even been attacking him. And to defend him, the egotistical, pushy chauvinist, who claimed to lead such a decadent lifestyle, who'd never offered her one ounce of sympathy, who had a harem of women up on the hill?

Heck, he was the son of a seadog he'd labeled himself. He'd seduced her without one word of love or commitment and expected more of the same action free and clear. Bree, you're not only a fool with a screw loose, you're an idiot, she chided herself.

Scratched and panting, Bree clapped her hands together to get rid of the dirt and stood up. Dusk was bringing in mosquitoes. Dusk was also, not surprisingly, bringing in darkness. A simple fifteen-minute stroll down her backyard, around the pond, and up the ravine to Hart's place had proved an obstacle course. She'd just

tumbled over a hidden rock. Much of his hillside was
made up of rocks and waist-high bramble bushes.

Rubbing her hands on the backs of her jeans, she
glanced up. Clouds had been rolling in all day, but had
waited until after dinner to start seriously rumbling overhead. A thick tangle of branches blocked her view of the
sky, but in the direction of Hart's house there were still
glimpses of lamplight. Way up there. *Still* way up there.

How Hart had scurried down to the pond so swiftly
was beyond her, particularly without being scratched to
bits and devoured by the man-eating mosquitoes. Irritably, she slapped at her neck, and then shook her head
in despair. Her neck felt bruised, and the mosquito was
still free, along with its supporting cast of thousands.

Digging her tennis shoe into a rocky crevice, she
stubbornly groped for another foothold. And then another. Sweat trickled down the back of her neck; a bramble grabbed her hair.

Her goal was to get to Hart before he showed up at
the cabin. Only why couldn't she have had the sense to
take the car and drive *around* the mountain?

Because she hadn't thought. Her mind had been totally
on getting this conversation over with. Her parents were
gone, and if they weren't completely in agreement with
her choices, at least there was peace between them. Bree
couldn't feel equally peaceful with herself until she'd
communicated with Hart.

The romp in bed had been nice, but there would be
no encores, though she had in mind telling him so tact-
fully. She'd rather gentled toward him, since he'd taken
that silly chivalrous role the day before with her parents,
but that really changed nothing. A flat-out sexual relationship with a man you argued with constantly the rest
of the time—it just wasn't her thing.

Thunder clapped overhead. Bree scowled. One fat
drop of rain made it through the umbrella of leaves above
and splashed on her nose.

Concentration was difficult. Mentally, she was trying to rehearse the proper words. *Hart, I don't think you were listening to me when we woke up yesterday morning, but I'm really not in the market for an affair. Shake hands on it?*

No, Bree.

Hi, Hart. Did you know I've been under an incredible amount of stress? I didn't think you did. You see, when your entire life is falling apart, occasionally you can be forgiven for spending a night . . . out of character. You see, that wasn't really me *you were sleeping with . . .*

Who was it then, Bree?

Well, maybe she didn't have a fully prepared speech yet, but how was she supposed to *think?* The rain was sneaking down, sliding into her hair and down her shirt.

His patio was cement, braced into the hillside with steel beams. She crawled under and then around it, and when she stepped onto the smooth flat white surface, a deluge of warm, utterly drenching rain greeted her. She lifted her face for a moment. Thanks, God. You couldn't have held off a few more minutes?

"You look more drenched than the rat the cat rejected," Hart drawled from the open glass doorway. "Couldn't you have waited another hour for me to come to you?"

Chapter Nine

BREE WHIRLED, her fingers scrambling to comb some kind of order to her rain-tangled hair. Hart had a brandy glass in his hand, the amber liquid shimmering in the fading light. He was dressed like a mountain man again, bare feet and dark jeans and a dark shirt open at the throat. Actually, that wasn't specifically mountain-man attire, but the image was there, in his mane of gold hair and cougar-fierce eyes that seared on hers straight through the darkness and rain.

"Let's get you inside and dry. Your parents gone?"

"They left for home. Listen, Hart—"

"Listen nothing. Let's get you into a hot shower."

Stepping cautiously over the threshold, she shook her head firmly. "I won't be here that long. I just wanted to tell—"

The thought was difficult to finish when her jaw was dropping. As swiftly as her eyes were taking in the incredible look of his living room, Hart was taking in the look of her bedraggled hair and wet clothes and unconscious shivering. "Shower *immediately.*"

Good intentions about staying cool didn't last long. "Hart, you have to stop ordering people around *some-*time," she started heatedly, but again lost her train of thought as she stared around her.

"You're absolutely right, Bree," Hart agreed, as he nudged her gently through the debris.

And there *was* debris. Somewhere at base level, there were the cream walls and matching carpet that the original owner must have put in. Maybe there was even a couch. It was hard to tell. *Everywhere* there were boxes and string and brown wrapping paper. Resting on top of one package was an enameled vase, preciously scrolled in teal blue and rose and gold. A two-foot-tall porcelain elephant was sitting on the floor. An Oriental carpet was half unrolled; Bree could just catch glimpses of its lusciously rich apricot and cream pattern. A harem of carved ivory dancing girls had been scattered on a table. More or less in the center of the floor she saw a legal pad and a pen.

"Where on earth did all this *come* from?"

"A delivery truck that wasted my *entire* afternoon. I'm surprised you didn't hear the noise and confusion at your place."

"I was out with my parents." She wanted to get another look, but, fingers dancing up and down her damp spine, Hart was coaxing her down a long hall, imperceptibly pushing. "Look. I am *not* going to take a shower," Bree said irritably.

"Okay, honey."

She glanced up at the rare malleable tone in his voice. He must have recently showered himself, because he smelled like soap. He looked tired, and she half frowned. Hart *never* looked tired. She didn't want him to look tired. She just wanted him safely on a different side of the globe from her, but when she parted her lips to start her tactful speech, he draped a hand loosely around her neck and pressed his warm cheek to her trembling cool one. He turned his face, and his lips stroked the spot where his cheek just had.

She'd drawn up such a wonderful set of determined goals over the past few hours. They dissipated like fog in early morning.

As she took a breath, her brain scrambled to salvage

a little common sense. His palm settled gently over her ribs, and pushed. One step back, and Hart had the space to close the door between them.

"I'll bring you some clothes," he called out. "When you're done just toss your stuff out. I'll throw 'em in the dryer."

Bree closed her eyes in exasperation. A moment later, she opened them to an ordinary bathroom in pale blue— ordinary except for the shiny brass dragon breathing fire at her from over the john.

Hart evidently liked his own things around him.

Her image confronted her in the mirror, and she frowned. The waif in the reflection was shivering violently. Anyone who looked as much like a dead rat as she did had a lot of presumption thinking she needed to call off an affair. And furthermore, there didn't seem any point in catching pneumonia for a few principles that would still be there a few minutes from now.

Besides, a shower would give her time to prepare more speeches. Flicking on the hot-water tap, she started stripping off her clothes. Ten minutes later, she turned off the pelting spray, dried off, and discovered Hart had been in and out in the meantime. A brush and hair dryer had been laid on the counter, and a man's soft plaid flannel shirt, in dark red and gray, was hanging from the dragon's nose.

With a rueful grimace, Bree snatched the shirt and outstared the dragon. "You don't seriously think this is all I'm going to wear around him, do you? You think I'm that stupid?"

The dragon failed to respond.

"I don't suppose you're willing to tell me where he keeps his jeans? Or what he's up to out there in the living room?"

The dragon wasn't willing.

"I get the nasty feeling you're trying to tell me I'm on my own here," she muttered glumly.

In minutes, her hair was dry, give or take a few damp curling strands around her neck. Inevitably, it looked flyaway soft after its soak in the rain. There weren't any rubber bands to tame it, although Hart's medicine cabinet yielded aspirin, toothpaste, and antacid tablets. She borrowed an antacid in lieu of a rubber band, gave her hair one last punishing brush in hopes it would stop looking like the mane of a wanton sixties flower child, and padded barefoot down the hall, Hart's shirt flapping around her bare thighs.

Silence. A tiny snooping foray down the hall later, and she discovered his bedroom. Her lips compressed the instant she walked in. Maybe if they shared one single value, maybe if her life weren't already totally in flux, maybe if he didn't constantly infuriate her, *maybe* she wouldn't have felt quite so definite about breaking off with him. His bedroom, though, just added another very good reason why she was headed for trouble if she didn't. A king-sized water bed. Natch. Scarlet satin sheets. A full-length mirror, and a really exquisite oil painting on the wall of a naked woman.

A clock tick-tocked from his bedside table. Briskly, Bree forced her eyes away from the reclining lady. The only reason she was invading this overgrown wolf's den was to find a pair of jeans. She found a half-dozen in the closet. Her eyes whisked back to the satin sheets as she donned a pair of white cords. Honestly. He was a womanizer to the core. He didn't *care* about her. There'd been a woman around, so he'd taken the opportunity; it was Bree's problem entirely that she'd given him the impression she was amenable to a fast, sweet fling. An impression she simply had to correct.

She bent over, cuffing the jeans four times. When she stood back up, she sighed. Unless she held up the pants, they weren't going to do much for her modesty; she could see clear down to her knees. She grabbed a belt, drew it through the loops, tucked her shirt in, and lashed the belt at its tightest notch.

Now, for battle.

Just outside the door to the living room, Bree took a deep breath, rapidly smoothed back her hair for the hundredth time, and pasted a serene smile on her face.

Hart clearly hadn't heard her approach. He was on the floor, straddling a huge box, attempting to balance a vase in one hand while scribbling on a legal pad with the other. He kept turning to study the exquisite ebony and gold vase. Setting it down, he reached absently for his brandy glass.

Bree frowned when he gulped down the contents of the glass in several long swigs. Before he'd finished swallowing, he was pouring himself another from a sweat-dripping silver pitcher on a tray on the floor. It appeared he'd already polished off half of the pitcher's contents.

Still, for a man who had to be inebriated, he handled the vase with delicate ... almost loving ... care. Momentarily diverted from her purpose, Bree jammed her hands in her pockets and crossed her bare feet in the doorway with a wisp of a smile on her face.

It was like watching a bear playing with butterflies. He looked so rugged and huge, and Lord knew his hands could move at the speed of light ... yet the way he touched each item he unwrapped, she could see all the tenderness the man was capable of. He wasn't smiling. He was concentrating; the furrow between his brows was testimony to that. She'd never seen Hart with his guard so far down. All masks had slipped; there was only a man working—and loving it.

She cleared her throat delicately. "Is this stuff from the import business you told me you hated so much?"

For a fleeting instant, Bree glimpsed a look of almost embarrassed wariness on his features, but his usual lazy smile immediately replaced it. "Once in a rare while I get stuck knuckling under like everyone else."

"Aren't you kind of a long way from where you normally do business?"

"I have three stores," Hart said absently, as he stuffed the vase back in the box, frowning as his eyes scanned the room. "San Francisco, Houston, New York... Sit anywhere, Bree, would you?... When there's a mess-up on quality—particularly with a new supplier—I get stuck sorting out the problem."

"No matter where you are, even on vacation?" Bree probed carefully.

"Whether I'm on vacation or not, my people would expect to be murdered if they accepted several thousand dollars' worth of merchandise that isn't up to snuff. They knew I'd want to see this, especially when we'd anticipated doing six-figure business with this particular supplier next year." Hart straightened up. "Not," he added swiftly, "that I care all that much about the business."

"Hmmm."

Hart's brows arched suspiciously. "What's that 'hmm' supposed to mean?"

"Why, nothing, Hart." For a man who didn't care all that much, just moments ago he'd looked as though his heart was in his work.

Avoiding her eyes suddenly, he motioned to the tray. "Ridiculous mess here, isn't it? Neatness isn't exactly my thing, and I figured I'd give you one more hour with your parents—there's another glass, Bree. Want a drink?"

"A *small* one," she said repressively.

He glanced up then, with an unholy grin. His eyes clung like tentacles to the loosely fitting shirt and baggy pants. He let out a roar. She scowled.

"How long will it take for my own clothes to dry?"

"Hours. Maybe years," he announced, and pushed aside a box to give her a space to sit on the floor. Leaning back, he poured a brandy snifter nearly full of amber liquid from the pitcher and handed it to her as she lowered herself, cross-legged, to the carpet next to him.

She took the glass but didn't sip. She was too busy worriedly watching Hart swallow another slug of brandy from his own glass. A strange confusion was settling in the pit of her stomach; something about Hart this evening was distinctly out of character, but overlaying that was a sharp disappointment that he was such a drinker. She had to give him credit for holding it well. His eyes on her were wide awake, full-of-devil dark blue, and glazed only with an intimate knowledge of her that seemed to transcend huge shirts and baggy pants.

Her mind groped for all her speeches, but her momentum seemed to have dissipated. Maybe plain curiosity was the problem. Certainly it wasn't that she got a kick out of just being with him. She flicked a spot of lint from her shirt. "So . . . what exactly are you doing here?"

"Nothing, really. Forget it, Bree. I was just playing around for a couple hours, anyway." Hart leaned back on an elbow, resting his brandy glass on his stomach. "Everything go all right with your father? I've spent a good twenty-four hours debating whether to go over there and make sure you had no more repercussions."

"Nothing happened with my father. Both my parents are wonderfully civilized people. You just happened to startle my father a little. Do you need any help with what you're doing?" *Now that's not what you're here for, Bree.* She buried her conscience's voice as she slid over to sneak a look at one of Hart's legal pads. The scribbled numbers took up ten pages. "Aren't you computerized, Hart?"

"Nope. I figure it's sort of like Custer's Last Stand. *Somebody's* got to hold out against the bytes and power surges that are taking over the world."

She chuckled, but then frowned. "You mean, you have to catalog everything that comes in *by hand?*" She shook her head, took another look at the room, and grabbed his pen. "You're going to have to tell me what you want me to do."

"Strip and do the dance of the seven veils?"

She touched her thumb to her nose and waggled her fingers. "You'll be up all night if you don't have some help," she scolded.

"You think I care about any of this stuff?"

"No, of course you don't," she said smoothly. "That's why you're doing it on your vacation."

Hart glared at her. "You were a lot easier to manage when you couldn't talk." He motioned to her still-full glass. "And you're letting a perfectly good drink go to waste."

He'd finished, she noticed, another one. Not touching her own, she finally bullied him into revealing his antiquated system of checking off numbers against the items and then the prices, which startled her. Hart's export-import stores obviously handled merchandise of very high quality, all hand-made or hand-carved items, his specialties being jade and ivory. She stopped checking only once, when she couldn't stop herself from reaching for the jade dragon in his hands. The carving was about six inches tall, with big, soulful eyes and a body the color of emeralds; he was whimsically mean-looking . . . but not really. "He reminds me of you," she said impishly.

"Thanks. Can we stop working soon?"

"Soon," she agreed. As soon as Hart wanted to, actually, but it was perfectly obvious he was worried about the shipment. Several things were cracked, producing massive scowls on his forehead and a muttered string of colorful expletives. Only when they came very close to the end did her throat feel dry. Thirstily, she reached for her glass.

She took a tiny sip and frowned, then took a bigger sip. "Hart," she said slowly.

"Hmmm."

"This is apple juice."

He glanced up. "If you want brandy, I probably have some in the kitchen somewhere."

"You *knew* I thought you were guzzling brandy like there was no tomorrow."

Hart pushed away a trail of wrappings and leaned back on his elbows with a grin. "Would you believe I do all my heavy drinking before lunch, just to be different?"

"No. And you deliberately led me to believe you drank *only* alcoholic beverages," she accused.

"When was this?" Hart asked with surprise.

"At the cabin. A few nights ago. You were yelling because I had no hooch or beer or anything you would conceivably drink—"

"Oh. That." Hart shrugged. "That was sort of a case of doing anything I could think of to keep you revved up, honey. Worked, didn't it? You slept like a log that night."

"What little sleep you let me have."

He grinned. "Come closer and let me check out the circles under your eyes *today*." He peered closer. "Good Lord. You've practically got ditches there. Who on earth kept you up *last* night?"

Bree choked on her apple juice. "No one kept me up *last* night. And don't try to avoid the subject."

"What subject?"

"You're a fraud," she said slowly. "You're not only a fraud, you're a *lousy* fraud. This . . . *stuff*." She waved her hands expressively over the room. "You led me to believe you never did any work at all, just traveled around the world and collected women."

"I *never* said I collected women."

Bree flushed, aware she'd put her own interpretation on some of his words here and there. "From the character sketch you gave me, I doubted very much that you even knew what your company imported—much less that you got directly involved in quality control."

"Sometimes, just for kicks, I stick my finger in to make sure everyone is doing a good job."

"Would you like me to tell you where you can stick your finger, Hart?"

He shook his head sadly. "If we could only regress about two days, when I had you well under my thumb, sexy and silent..."

"Do you have a family?" Bree swung her legs under her, her fists on her knees.

"How did *they* get into this? Of course I have a family." He added mildly, "What members didn't disown me in my younger days."

"Specifically, did your mother survive those younger days?"

"Mom? She's a brick."

Bree had to severely repress laughter. "And your father. The one who despaired you'd ever turn out a productive human being?"

"Dad was a very productive human being. He had me, didn't he? And three more. He's more into being happily retired than reproducing these days. None of the rest of the siblings, alas, inherited my incredible good looks. Come on over here, Bree."

When she failed to move, he tugged at her pantlegs. The harder he pulled, the more the jeans were in danger of slipping down from her hips, in spite of the belt. Bree batted at his fingers, but Hart's hands were bigger than hers. He wasn't content until she was sitting facing him, with his legs over hers and a lazy grin within kissing distance. "We've been talking too much," he informed her gravely. "Let's get you polluted on apple juice, so I can have my way with you."

She sighed, loudly. "You're not going to have your way with me, Hart; that isn't why I came here, and did they all turn out as badly as you did? The siblings, I mean?" She was determined to finish the conversation. As far as she could tell, every single thing he'd ever told her about himself had been a lie. In one sense, she felt enraged, in another like laughing, and in another . . . she wasn't at all sure what she was feeling. Danger, at being close to him. And loving being close. And fear that she was coming to conclusions too fast.

It was kind of mind-boggling, watching the transformation of Hart from irresponsible globe-trotter to dedicated businessman. From an alcoholic to a man hooked on apple juice. From articulate cynic to secret softie.

And Hart's eyes held navy-blue glints that kept trying to beguile her, even as he impatiently answered her questions. "Most of them turned out worse. John's been in law school for about fifty years now. He *loves* going to school. Jennifer married a doctor, which sounds good enough except that they had to buy into a practice, and with a baby on the way—"

"They were broke?"

"After so many years of medical school? Hell, they didn't have a crumb in the cupboard. Eric's the worst. He decided a few years ago to go back to nature. He has a little farm in Vermont. Very picturesque. Very, very picturesque mortgage. They charge gold bullion for land there, you know."

"Nope, I didn't."

"And Eric's got two kids besides. Twins. Two years old and so damned cute—not that I like kids," he added hastily. "But when you're stuck with a couple of nephews, what the heck."

"You adore them," Bree said flatly.

"Maybe," Hart hedged.

"And you've been obligated to help your brothers and sisters financially."

"They're all in a hurry to get off my hands. A few more years and I can be *really* irresponsible. Anyway, this conversation has taken a kind of boring turn." He smiled in such an innocent, disarming way, just before his fingers pulled at the open throat of her shirt and he ducked his head for a view. "You know, I really think this is one of the world's scenic wonders. Ever seen the Taj Mahal?"

"*No*. Hart—"

"Lots of white marble, a few fountains. Domed tops. I like your domed tops better. Talk about your architectural wonders." Thirty seconds later, he had whisked all the wrapping paper away, lowered a startled Bree to the carpet, and was straddling her. One of his fingers was busy with the buttons of her shirt as he grinned. "I know a great game for domed tops."

"You weigh at least a ton, and I didn't come here for this."

"Now, Bree." He flipped open two buttons, in spite of her hands chasing after him. "To hell with domed tops. Ice-cream cones. That's really what they remind me of. Do you lick your ice-cream cones from the top or the sides?"

His tongue flicked over a nipple. The helpless laughter rippling through Bree abruptly died. His soft tongue strayed down to the side of one breast, lapping at the circumference as if he were indeed savoring vanilla ice cream. Or maybe chocolate. Or maybe wild cherry.

"Unlike ice-cream cones, the more you lick, the *less* they disappear. Have you noticed that phenomenon, Bree? They're swelling up," he whispered. His eyes lifted distractedly to hers. "Also, they're not at all cold. One might even go so far as to say—"

"*Hart*. Sex is a serious business. Do you have a straightjacket I could conveniently put on you for the next five minutes?"

He shook his head. "Honey, you're such a mental mess. Who on earth gave you your sex education, anyway? A nerd? Sex is *fun*. I thought we covered all this two nights ago." He glanced down at what his hand was covering and started chuckling. "We did. Cover this. Extensively."

"You still have work to do," Bree said desperately. How had things gotten out of hand so fast? Maybe her prepared speeches were in a mental rejection pile, and maybe they belonged there, but she still didn't want an affair based only on sex . . . even if her heart was kicking in approval at a thundering rate.

"All work and no play makes Johnny a dull boy."

"A stitch in time saves nine," she shot back.

"An apple a day keeps the doctor away."

Bree frowned up at him. "What do apples have to do with anything?"

"I thought you wanted to quote proverbs."

She closed her eyes disgustedly. A mistake. Hart promptly leaned over to kiss them. Lips softer than silk brushed the delicate flesh of her eyelids, then grazed her cheekbone, then burrowed into her rain-softened hair.

He was doing it again, she thought dismally. Making her smile, making her feel intensely desired, making her believe there could be absolutely nothing more right or delightful than fooling around with him. Ice-cream cones, damn him.

His lips teased the corner of her mouth, nipping and gently biting until she parted her own. He waited then, eyes soft and silent on hers before he moved. His tongue flicked at the entrance of her lips, then thrust in, filling every secret moist corner. He withdrew it, then thrust in again. And again. With a helpless, almost angry little murmur, Bree surged closer, rubbing her hips against his, a capitulation that she could no more have helped than breathing.

"Honey." Hart raised his mouth. Not far. "I know you're hot for my bod, but try to slow down a little. I'm not going anywhere. I promise."

If it weren't for the dance in his eyes, she would have killed him. Actually, it was probably because of the dance in his eyes that she wanted to. "Manning. Hasn't one single woman in your life ever taught you to shut up?"

"Nope. That's going to be up to you."

Bree took a breath, a vulnerable softness suddenly haunting her eyes. "You know, the only reason I came over here was to tell you I didn't want any more of this."

"Tell me, then," Hart encouraged. Putting an elbow on both sides of her face, he cupped his chin in his hands, giving her all his encouraging attention.

"I just *did*. Affairs just aren't my thing, and I really don't think getting involved with you is . . . wise," she ended lamely.

"Honey, you seem to be terribly confused. We *are* involved. And you like it just fine. You've been trying not to laugh for the better part of half an hour."

She bit her lip. "Hart, stop making this so hard—"

His eyebrow flickered up. "You're the one who made it so hard, honey." He shifted his hips expressively.

"Hart."

"You're right. Let's get serious, Bree." Using an arm for leverage, he vaulted off her and, when standing, reached for her hand. She took it and raised herself up beside him, her lips still throbbing faintly from the pressure of his. The suddenly disappointed look in his eyes startled her. "If you really want to get serious that fast, we can move immediately to the water bed. I'd planned on a little lengthy foreplay, but if you're that hot, honey—"

"Could you just *once* stop talking?"

"Will *you* stop thinking so damn much? Arms up for my Valentino act." He raised her arms himself, hooked them around his neck, and slid one arm around her and the other under her thighs. "This is the carry-off-to-the-sunset scene. Although it's my best guess that guy ended up in traction," he murmured, just before his mouth crushed down, obliterating any chance of her reply.

Chapter Ten

TALK, TALK, TALK. Bree had never met a man who talked as much as Hart did. From the moment she met him, there'd been only one way to shut him up. With her arms loosely around his neck, she pressed a kiss on his mouth, effectively ending his incessant, annoying chatter.

Whom do you think you're fooling? Bree, you're in trouble again, warned a small voice in her head. She banished the voice. As he carried her down the dark hall, her lips nuzzled his neck, trailing up so that her teeth could gently nip at his ear. Eyes closed, she let her fingers grope for the buttons on his shirt.

Hart chuckled, murmuring something approving she didn't quite hear, and then bent down to sink smooth, warm lips onto hers. They had to stop then, because Hart leaned back against the wall, and when the kiss was over his breathing was different and his pace had quickened toward the bedroom.

Her heart picked up a murmur en route. A love murmur. If Hart thought he'd distracted her into this seduction, he was completely mistaken. She was being pushed into nothing. She knew darn well she was asking to be hurt—getting oneself involved with a womanizer wasn't wise; he'd never seriously talked about anything permanent and undoubtedly had nothing more than a summer fling in mind. Tough. He made her laugh; he made her feel like screaming; he made her throw things; he made her feel *alive,* and every nerve ending now pulsed with wanting him.

But to toss out a whole lifetime of sane, rational behavior for one wild fling at love? *Yes,* murmured the exuberant voice in her head. *Yes yes yes.* What choices do you have beyond going back to being dependable old Bree again in a few more weeks? This is your chance. Hart seems to take for granted that you're an uninhibited wanton who throws caution to the winds; *be* that wildly passionate woman, just once; be wanton, just once. There'll never be anyone like Hart in your life again...

She meant the words; she felt the emotions; she ached with the richness of freedom released in her soul... but all of her bravery dissipated in the doorway to the bedroom. Hart paused, suddenly looking down at her with dark, too-far-seeing eyes. "What's wrong?" he whispered.

"Nothing's wrong." How could he have noticed that tiny lick of tension in her spine?

"Something is." Still carrying her, he nudged her cheek with his when she tried to duck her head.

"I was just worrying that you were going to break your neck, toting me around like this."

"Bree." There was a lot of gentle scolding in that single syllable.

She lowered her eyes, leaning her cheek to his shoulder. "Could we..." She hesitated. "Hart, could we go somewhere else? Please?"

"You mean, somewhere besides the bedroom?"

"It's just...water beds and satin sheets...it's not my thing. I feel..." She hesitated again.

"Silly?"

She let out a breath and gave a half-smile. "Inhibited," she confessed with embarrassment. He undoubtedly did this with dozens of women. That was, of course, his prerogative, but that bedroom made her think of his dozens of other women.

"Inhibited? That'll be a cold day in hell."

"Hart," she reproved.

Slowly, he released her until her feet touched the floor, but he didn't let her go. Thoughtfully, he brushed her hair from her face and smoothed one fingertip over her cheek in a soft, silent caress. Gently, he leaned his forehead to hers. "Honey. I bought those sheets the day before yesterday. To seduce you on."

"Oh."

"They're slippery, I discovered last night. So slippery they make the pillows skim onto the floor as if they're on a toboggan run. They're also cold. Takes forever for a body to warm them up. Even so . . ."

"You want to try them?"

His lips just touched her forehead, and his voice came out languid and slow. "The kitchen table's fine by me, honey. So is right here on the hall carpet. I thought the lady might feel . . . luxurious. Pampered. You need some pampering, Bree."

"No, I don't."

"Yes, you do."

She sighed. Knowing Hart, he'd argue all night. "But the . . ."

"Water bed? Great for a bad back, but one does get the feeling that isn't why the owner put it in." Hart pulled her arms back up around his neck, and then dipped his head to nuzzle the curve of her shoulder. "You think I've set up a swinging singles scene in there, honey. Won't wash. I just rented the place, and I outgrew one-night stands about ten years ago. Traveling—alone—can be the loneliest life there is."

Hart's eyes pinned hers, a dark blue that was fathomless and intense. There was a gravity to his features that begged her to trust, to believe. With a small smile, she touched her finger to his lips. "Hart, you're totally destroying the decadent image you've built up."

For once Hart didn't smile back. "And is that an image you want, Bree?"

She stared up at him in confusion.

"I think it is," he said quietly. "I don't know what hurt you so badly, honey, but I think you've convinced yourself that all you want is a wild, free affair. A fling where there are no consequences and you only have to open up your heart so far . . . You're wrong, Bree. You're wrong as hell. But if that's all you're looking for, I'll be damned if you'll have that affair with anyone else."

"Hart . . ." He was implying she was using him, and he was wrong, terribly wrong. Surely he was wrong. Hart was the one who had a harem; Bree had never been capricious. Hart had made all the first moves, never Bree. And he was the one who'd deliberately built up the decadent image . . . but it was a fraud; she saw now just how much of a fabrication that was. Uncertain green eyes fluttered up to his. "Look, I never . . ."

"Don't talk," he murmured. "Talk's never as honest as touch. If you want wild, believe me I can give you wild, honey . . ." His mouth stole closer, and when he'd claimed her lips he never once let them go.

Thunder exploded in the night, and Bree instinctively curled closer to Hart's warm body. The clock next to her ticked past three. Raindrops gushed down the windowpanes; swords of lightning dueled in the darkness outside.

She couldn't sleep.

The pillows were on the floor. They'd slid there hours before; the satin sheets were just as slippery as Hart had said. Beneath her, the water bed cradled the two of them in a cocoon of warmth and softness, and every once in a while she could see the reflection of lightning on the full-length mirror by the bed.

She kept staring at that mirror, seeing images in it that weren't there. Images of Hart poised over her, his body dark gold and damp, the rhythm of his limbs as he made love to her. Her own image, with her throat arched back, her breasts raised brazenly for his touch; the image of a stranger, a beautifully sensual woman with slumberous eyes and a sleek, proud body, who twined around her mate with all the primitive desire of an Eve.

She'd never meant to look in the mirror, any more than she'd meant to enjoy the satin sheets or the water bed. She'd felt somewhat inhibited at first, her tension sparked by Hart's disturbing words. Only he'd stripped off her clothes and never given her the chance to think, and these . . . sensations . . . had just kept coming. And it wasn't the sensuality of satin that set it off; it was the sensuality of the man. Hart, so fiercely passionate, teasing her and whispering and coaxing . . .

So beautiful. Whenever he touched her she felt so incredibly beautiful, and she wanted to say, This really isn't me, you know, Hart. It just happens when I'm with you . . .

A warm palm suddenly slid under her arm, over her ribs and behind her, very sneakily, making her smile in the darkness. "Still not sleepy?" Hart scolded groggily. "Not nightmares, though, Bree?"

"Not nightmares at all," she affirmed, and snuggled closer.

"We've lost our pillows."

She chuckled softly. "You warned me about the satin sheets."

His palm made slow concentric circles on her spine, and only gradually moved up to sift through her hair. "The lady liked the satin sheets," he said with satisfaction. "She also liked the mirror."

"She *never* looked."

"Oh, yes, she did." Even in the darkness, she could see the crooked smile on his lips as he leaned up on one elbow. His eyes were luminous, and suddenly there was no smile. "You trust me, Bree, did you know that?"

She parted her lips, but said nothing.

"Trust isn't a measure of how long and how well you've known someone. It's an instinct. You could have kicked me out of the cabin that first time, Bree. You could have stopped me from making love to you with a single word. Several times I made you very, very angry, but your trust was still there. We didn't have sex, honey; we didn't even make love." He bent over to kiss her forehead, then her lips. "We touched the stars. A woman doesn't give that way unless there's a very special trust."

"I never said I didn't trust you," she countered softly.

"You didn't have to." His thumb rubbed the edge of her bottom lip. "I want to know about your nightmares," he said quietly. "I want to know about the haunted look that sometimes comes into your eyes; I want to know what happened that was so terrible you couldn't talk about it. Can you trust out loud yet, Bree?"

She didn't answer. There was a foolish lump in her throat, and her eyes blurred with the faintest glistening of tears. She couldn't tell him about Gram; she couldn't tell anyone about Gram, but she felt like shouting that she'd given him more than she'd given any other man. Wasn't it enough?

He wanted too much; from the beginning he'd wanted too much. And even if she could have told him about Gram . . . she had to draw a line somewhere. She'd never shared her feelings easily; with Hart she felt more vulnerable than she'd ever felt before, and Hart's nature was so clearly to capture and claim and possess . . . but when he moved on? When she had to go back to being "just Bree" again? "Dammit, what do you want from me?" she said.

"Watch," he answered. His eyes gleamed down at her for just a moment before the magic started again. He seduced, with lips and tongue and the stroke of his hands. Not again, she was so sure it couldn't happen again, but layers of civilized inhibitions seemed to peel off in that velvet darkness; the sheer power of woman rose up in her like a devilish fire.

Thunder crashed outside; wind whipped leaves against the windows. The darkness held mystery; Hart's eyes refused to close, holding hers, even as his hands molded her breasts, slid down the warm flesh of her stomach, and cupped that core of mysterious yearning within her.

Almost against her will, her own hands grew bolder. Her legs wound around him; she rubbed against him, and her lips started a ceaseless whispered trail everywhere she could reach, on his shoulders and arms, on his throat and chest, up to his lips. Such a terrible, restless heat; her body was very warm, yet the sheets were cool beneath her, cool and slippery.

"Now," she murmured. "Please, now, Hart . . ." What was he waiting for?

"You want me inside you?"

Yes."

"Then show me," he whispered. "Show me, Bree." Languidly, he shifted both of them, until she was no longer beneath him but on top. "Make love to me." He raised his head to reclaim her swollen mouth; the kiss was fierce, and his hands glided down the length of her in urgent encouragement.

Still, she felt swamped by a terrible feeling of inadequacy. She would die before she failed Hart as a lover. "I haven't . . ." she whispered awkwardly.

"Show me what you want, Bree. It's so easy. So easy to love, honey. Just reach out . . ."

Go after what you want; it was what he'd always said; something she'd always found so terribly hard to do, and she'd never been assertive in loving. He refused to understand how difficult it was for her. Instead, he kept murmuring encouragements she could barely hear, promising her wonderful, terrible things, and with long, soothing strokes he coaxed her body to perch over his, until she could no longer stand the long, torturous teasing. She took him inside her, trembling like a leaf, feeling the first promised rush of release as her thighs enfolded him, the hollow of her filled.

As a reward, Hart leaned forward to softly lap at her breasts, his hands cradling her hips. She went still then, content to have him take over again, but he whispered, "I'm right here with you. Go with the fire, Bree—don't you dare stop now."

He kept saying her name and his hands were everywhere, on her hips, on her breasts, and she started the ancient rhythm because . . . she had to. Because Hart's whole body vibrated with need and because there was something incredibly exciting in watching him take fire when she moved, when she tightened her limbs just so, when he made it so very clear that she was doing everything . . . right.

A once-shy Bree turned exultant, bold, learning how to please him, testing the rhythms that made his eyes darken and his hips tense and his hands move restlessly over her flesh. His body was hers, for this hour. He belonged to her, and that was a heady, sweet power, purely feminine, deliciously exhilarating. She was loving him, not being loved, and for that instant it was utterly, totally enough in itself. Then, in the lushness of giving, her thighs suddenly tightened around him and her spine arched back and a sweet shower of silver flooded everywhere, within, without, all over.

Moments later, Hart tugged her down to collapse against him. His breathing was still rough, so was hers; their bodies were damp and warm. "You asked me," he murmured, "what I wanted from you, Bree. Just that, love. For you to see, for you to shout it, that you're a beautiful, passionate woman, capable of unbelievable giving, strong enough to demand what she wants in her life as well. Look at you," he whispered.

She curled around him and snuggled to his chest,

replete and exhausted and ignoring his utterly foolish demand. She loved him so much she hurt.

"You can stop *grinning* at me as if you'd won a war," Bree scolded.

Hart lifted the spoon from his cornflakes bowl and wagged it at her like a finger. He hadn't shaved, and in between the blond layers of stubble on his chin was an extremely smug grin that had been there ever since they'd awakened that mor—afternoon. "Eat your cereal, sexy. Heaven knows you burned up enough calories last night. You need your strength."

Bree sputtered mentally, but not for long. What was the use? Hart had probably been born irreverent. Digging into her cornflakes, she passed him the front section of the morning paper, and buried her smile behind the women's section.

Truth was, she felt the silly urge to sing this mor—afternoon. Turn cartwheels. Skydive. The mood was irrational, but there it was. Under the kitchen table, she crossed her bare feet, lifted them comfortably onto Hart's lap, and turned the page to Erma Bombeck.

Hart finished his cereal. He reached for his coffee with one hand, while his other palm stole under the table to stroke her bare instep. Ticklish, she squirmed, scowling over the top of the paper at him. Hart *refused* to be restful this morning.

"Where we going for dinner tonight?" he asked her.

She blinked. "I wasn't aware we were going anywhere."

"Certainly we are. I had in mind a little steak over a fire at the pond, around six. I'll bring the steak; you bring the marshmallows."

Unreasonably disappointed that he wasn't proposing anything for the afternoon, Bree nodded. "All right."

Hart chuckled. "You're slipping, honey."

"Pardon?"

"Even two days ago, you were still on the get-out-of-my-life kick. Do I sense a slight mellowing in your attitude?" There was a peculiarly intense light in his eyes in spite of his lazy drawl; she couldn't read it.

Bree shrugged, returning to Erma Bombeck. "I admit you've kind of grown on me." Green eyes twinkled at him. "Kind of like a fungus." Hart slid his nail down the bottom of her foot. Bree jerked, bumped her knee under the table, reclaimed both limbs, and tucked them safely under her chair. "A more-trouble-than-you're-worth fungus," she said darkly.

He leaned both elbows on the table. "But you weren't quite so nervous waking up next to me this morning. Notice that?"

"Do you really want an answer to that?" Swinging out of the chair, she reached for the breakfast dishes. Before she'd even carried them to the sink, he was behind her, deftly stealing the bowls from her hands and swinging her around.

"I really hate to say this," he whispered, "but I think I'm getting through to the lady."

"You are," she agreed, and perched up on tiptoe to kiss him.

Her action seemed to take him back, for the brooding midnight darkness left his eyes and a crooked smile touched his mouth. "What was that for?" He sounded just the slightest bit wary, as though he'd just opened Pandora's box and wasn't sure what the contents were going to be.

"Honesty, Hart," she said softly. Sincerity shone out in the vulnerability in her clear eyes. "You drive me nuts," she admitted, "but you've also done something special for me. You *are* someone special to me. I'm not holding you to anything, Hart; I want you to understand that. You're perfectly free when you want to be free."

His smile abruptly died. "You're a failure," he murmured, "at playing it light and breezy, Bree. Don't try."

At the cabin, just before six, she was still trying. Her emerald-green blouse was tied at the ribs; white jeans led down to a frivolous pair of green sandals; and her hair was pulled back with cheerful green yarns. "Light and breezy" was the message; she even applied mascara with a light and breezy touch, which made the black stuff smudge all over her eyes.

Muttering darkly, Bree wiped off her smile and then the smudges, starting over again with her makeup. The crooked mirror in the loft didn't help, mostly because it inevitably made one cheek look higher than the other, and she was fairly sure she wasn't made that way. Picnic-type dinners didn't call for a lot of makeup anyway, which was why she was careful to use every effective brand in her drawer, but so imperceptibly that Hart wouldn't notice.

She didn't want him to think she cared; she just wanted to look devastatingly casual.

Finishing up with blusher, she pulled the throat of her blouse open and generously splashed her chest with the most wicked perfume she'd created yet. Heck, the smell would dissipate in the open air anyway. Light and breezy, she echoed, as she stepped back and regarded her image in the mirror.

No good. The lady in the mirror had her heart in her eyes. Bree practiced another fake devil-may-care smile. So she adored the man. So what? So in time she would go back home like good, responsible Bree, and he would return to his harem on the hill. The trick was not to take it all too seriously, just to get into this business of having a wild affair and simply enjoy. Hundreds of women did it all the time.

A fine philosophy for a hedonist. By nature, she'd

never been much of a hedonist. "You're on the way to getting hurt very badly," she scolded the braless Gypsy in the mirror.

The Gypsy practiced a careless shrug. *Oh, stop it, Bree.*

But Bree didn't want to stop it. The screw that had snuck loose when Gram died? She'd tighten it up in time; she'd go back and dust her apartment and pay her bills and find a nine-to-five job and *behave* herself again. But not yet. Her heart thumped helplessly in her chest when she heard the rap on the door downstairs.

After running the brush through her hair one last time, she skipped down the stairs. Grabbing the bag of marshmallows from the counter, she opened the door with a winsome grin of anticipation that abruptly died.

Hart was on her doorstep, but not alone. Next to him stood Marie, her one-time boss, dressed in a simple sharkskin dress and white sandals, her blond hair sleekly pinned in a French coil. Marie was not beautiful and never would be, but she carried off the image of a self-sufficient, independent woman without effort. Because she was one.

Bree promptly felt as underdressed as an orphan. Her eyes whipped up to Hart. In navy cotton cords with a stark white shirt, he dwarfed both of them. He was looking at Marie, and they were both laughing so hard that neither of them had heard her open the door.

A sock in the gut would have been kinder.

Bree knew Marie . . . so well. Just as Marie had been very good at stuffing Bree in the back office for the last five years, she was an expert at taking the limelight herself. Since Bree hated limelight and had always acknowledged Marie's unquestionably effective skills with people, for a very long time they had gotten on remarkably well. Even after Bree had handed in her resignation, there were no hard feelings between them. Bree's boss used her, yes, but the only fault had been in Bree, for letting that happen. Marie couldn't help who she was.

And Marie was unquestionably a self-assured, successful woman. Exactly the type that Hart had said appealed to him when they first met. Really, Bree thought brightly, Hart and Marie were a natural pair, a matched set. It was amazing that she'd ever thought he could be permanently attracted to anyone as serious and nonflamboyant as good old Bree...

"Bree!" Marie turned with a startled little laugh and threw her arms around Bree in an exuberant hug. "Surprised?"

"I—yes." *Total shock* was sort of a synonym for *surprise,* wasn't it?

"Your dad called me yesterday, and when I heard you had your speech back, I just couldn't resist coming! I knew you never meant to resign, Bree. You weren't yourself, and I was just so *glad* that things have turned out all right for you again." She nodded with a special smile for Hart. "I was just telling this neighbor of yours that I'd planned to take you out to dinner, so we could talk. I can't stay; my return flight's at midnight, and Hart says he knows this little restaurant—"

"Fine." Bree smiled brilliantly. The sensations were all familiar, being squeezed into Marie's self-imposed schedules.

"I was just telling him that you're the best systems analyst in the business. And that I had to be half to blame for your taking off to this godforsaken place. You were working too hard, Bree, and I'm totally responsible for giving you a workload the size of a mountain..." Marie, turning, slipped on the wooden step.

Hart grabbed her arm. Bree's eyes were fixed on Hart's long brown fingers clutching Marie's white sleeve, on the fluttering smile Marie cocked up at him, on the closeness of their two bodies and the late-afternoon sun pouring down on them. "It's a little rustic for me around here," Marie admitted with a little laugh to Hart. "I have to admit that I'm strictly an indoor-sports enthusiast."

Ah, yes, Bree thought bleakly, feeling like a reluctant third as they headed for Hart's rented New Yorker. It hadn't taken long for Marie to fall. Around Hart, it wouldn't take any woman long to fall.

And Hart wasn't fighting it very hard, if he'd already decided on a restaurant, if they were already on a comfortable first-name basis, if they'd been laughing like old friends after only a few minutes' acquaintance.

"The steaks will wait for another night," Hart murmured as he handed Bree into the car. She glanced up once at him, to glimpse a cool, unfathomable expression in his eyes that she'd never seen before. "Systems analyst, is it?" he muttered. "I'm just beginning to realize what else you were stingy about telling me. You had quite a boss, didn't you, Bree?"

Bree ducked her head, feeling miserable. He didn't have to *say* it.

". . . but I wouldn't miss this evening for the world. Get in, talkative Charlie. Let's find out what else you haven't told me." The car door shut resoundingly in her ear.

Bree turned to Marie with a smile that was beginning to feel glued on. Hart was irritated with her—she didn't have the least idea why. Marie was clearly unworried by Bree's presence as a third party, Bree understood very clearly why; she had never been competition for Marie.

A trip to the Yukon seemed preferable to the evening ahead. Heck, Bree thought wildly, why get picky? She'd settle for Antarctica.

Chapter Eleven

"I STARTED CONTEC on a shoestring about five years ago. There was just myself, Bree, and Allen Spencer—but we got rid of Allen within two months, didn't we, Bree?" Marie's eyes flickered briefly on Bree before zooming instantly back to Hart. "Dead weight, that man. Bree could pick up a new system ten times faster than he could. But it wasn't just that. When a company calls with trouble, you have to send someone who can understand not only their computer system but their specific problems as well, whether it's a manufacturing difficulty or an unreliable accounting organization—"

"I'm afraid you're going too fast," Hart interrupted, leaning back against the red leather booth with a smile. "Computers are half Greek to me. From what you're saying, can I assume that a systems analyst is a kind of troubleshooter?"

"Exactly—at least in our approach. Contec sells expertise in technology, not the equipment itself. You'd be surprised how many companies invest thousands of dollars in computers and then can't make the system work for them."

"So Bree goes in . . ."

"And educates. Or trains. Or revamps their system. Or custom-programs . . ."

A black-suited waiter brought a second bottle of wine. Bree tuned the conversation out and tipped the newly filled glass to her lips, delighted with the way the wine slid smoothly down her throat. Amazing, how suddenly fascinated Hart was by the subject of computers. And Marie had been delighted to educate him all through dinner.

Marie gave another scintillating, high-pitched laugh, and Bree downed the rest of her wine. To be honest— though she really had no interest in honesty at the moment—she hadn't been ignored. Hart had turned to glare at her about every minute and a half, and Marie had waxed poetic on the subject of Bree's ability on the job. Bree knew Marie was trying to seduce her back to work. Why Hart was so irritated she had no idea, except that he was probably astounded she would leave such a charming and attractive employer and such a "plush" job. Marie was good at making long hours and tedium sound delightful.

Bree had been too busy during dinner to join in the conversation anyway. After the second glass of wine, she'd been simply fascinated watching Marie bounce back and forth from manipulative boss to a lady who helplessly batted her eyelashes. It was really an interesting phenomenon; all Hart had to do was breathe and Marie's laughter trilled out like a chorus of "Take Me."

Come on, Bree, you knew he was the kind to attract women, in the plural. She reached for the bottle of wine and found Hart had unobtrusively shifted it to the opposite side of the table. The cup of coffee that had just miraculously appeared in front of her was a poor substitute, but it gave her something to do with her hands, stirring black swirls into black swirls.

"So your company is based on field work, with a willingness to show up day or night no matter what the problem is . . ." Hart continued.

"Exactly." Marie shook her head prettily, her dancing eyes never leaving Hart's face. "Bree can tell you how often she's been called in the middle of the night by a manager who supervises a night shift..." She shrugged. "When they need their payroll ready by seven in the morning, someone has to be there to make sure it gets down. That's been our reputation from the beginning— to be there when called, day or night. Actually, Bree sometimes worked forty-eight hours at a stretch—"

"Forty-eight hours at a stretch," Hart echoed flatly.

Bree caught the little darts Hart's eyes sent her again. She sent him back a brilliant smile, just for kicks, and reached for her coffee.

"You have to be willing to stay on the job until the problem's solved. That's partly why Bree's so fantastic. My dependable Bree," Marie said affectionately. "Of course, we've expanded since those early beginnings; I have five more people on my staff now. Bree trained them all, and I can remember last January when we had two out with flu; I told Bree I didn't see how we could possibly manage, but of course—"

"She managed very well," Hart finished smoothly.

"I can always count on Bree. I swear, I'd have to have two more people without her." Marie smiled, flashing her eyes up at Hart as he leaned over to refill her wineglass again.

Hart smiled back, very lazily. "But I'm sure you share some of the work load in the field yourself, Marie."

Marie chuckled. "I hate to admit this," she whispered conspiratorially, "but I'd be totally lost in the field. Bree does that kind of work better than anyone. My job is to sell the services we have to offer, but if I had to deliver the real nuts and bolts, I'm afraid I'd be a total failure."

Marie clearly expected Hart to empathize with her, but Hart, at just that instant, dropped his smile. "I would say you were a natural success," Hart said icily, "at selling *Bree*."

Bree stiffened, even more so as Marie stood up with a little laugh. "Come on, Hart. There's an empty dance floor out there, and you must be sick of listening to me talk about business. Between Bree and me, we'll keep your feet moving for a while."

Bree noticed the quick flash of annoyance in his eyes, replaced almost instantly with a cool mask. Seconds later, he escorted Marie to the pocket-sized dance floor. The pianist was playing an old torch song, and Bree watched Marie's fingers seductively climb up Hart's shoulders, her head tilting back, her lips looking miraculously moistened.

Hart danced like a robot, amazing Bree. She hadn't figured for him for a disco kid, but the music was sensual and she knew well that he had a most incomparable sense of . . . rhythm. And his mouth, she noted, was going a mile a minute. The lady in his arms wasn't getting kissed; she was getting grilled. Poor Marie.

Bree almost smiled, but couldn't. A clear-cut attack of jealousy would have been easy enough to handle, but she could hardly blame Hart because women fell all over him. She'd done the same, hadn't she?

And the entire evening had opened up a can of worms. Hart's comment about Marie "selling Bree" hurt—and badly. If he'd meant it as a compliment to Marie, Bree took it as an insult to herself—one that she, unfortunately, deserved. She *had* let Marie sell her, for five long years. Marie had never demanded; rather, she'd functioned as a football coach. You can do more, Bree; I know you can handle this one, Bree; imagine what this project will do for our reputation, darling; win this one for me . . .

And she had. Because she was by nature responsible and motivated by security, and because she had always found it so very hard to say no to people.

A cold fog surrounded Bree from nowhere. For days, she hadn't thought of Gram. Once the nightmares were over and her speech had returned, she'd assumed that the trauma was over. The sudden fierce panic in her heart informed her that it wasn't. All she could think of was that Gram would never have sat here like this. She'd never have stayed in a job where she was being used. She'd never have fallen in love with a man who drew every feminine eye. She'd never have just stood by passively and let things happen to her...

The music ended, and the two were wending their way around tables, coming toward her. Bree barely noticed. As if her hand were attached to another woman's body, Bree found herself suddenly picking up her purse to depart.

"Bree?" Marie cocked her head in question.

"What's wrong?" Hart's voice was quiet, an echo of a dozen intimate love words between them.

But then, Hart was very good with love words. He was brilliant with women, period. "I'm going home," Bree said brightly, and swung her hips out of the booth. Hart's fingers curled on her wrist, but she shook herself free. She couldn't breathe. There was just no air in the place, and Hart's touch hurt just a little too much.

A waiter was pushing a cart of desserts between the tables. She dodged him, dragging a hand through her hair. Hart was demanding the bill; she heard that, and Marie's chatter. She knew that the pianist had started another song, and that the carpet was a patterned black and red. Such silly details struck her when for a moment she was utterly disoriented as to the location of the exit. There had to be an exit; they'd come in somewhere—

The door was ridiculously heavy; once she was outside, she hauled great gulps of night air into her lungs. Her hands were shaking—silly. Nothing was wrong. She was awake; there was no nightmare. She was standing in a parking lot filled with cars; a crescent moon cradled a bevy of stars; a warm breeze wisped around her on an absolutely lovely night... and her hands wouldn't stop trembling.

"We'll have you home in twenty minutes." Hart's baritone was quiet and sure, coming from behind her even as he placed a supportive arm on her shoulder.

She shrugged it off, vaulting for the car.

"Bree? My goodness, darling, what happened? I was just telling Hart that I wanted you to take more time off. You deserve a vacation, so make it as long as you—"

Bree whirled to face Marie. "I'm not coming back," she said crisply. "I gave you my resignation; you knew that before you came here."

"Of course I did," Marie said soothingly, even as she glanced at Hart. The look was "meaningful" and made Bree almost physically ill. "But you can't give up an excellent job on a whim, darling. I know you don't mean it. After you've had a little more rest—"

"I've had tons of rest, and I've decided I'd rather wait on tables for a living." She'd reached Hart's car, and grabbed the back-seat door handle.

"You can't mean that—"

"You have something against waitresses?" Bree frowned at Hart. He'd removed her hand from the door handle of the back seat and was firmly trying to maneuver her into the front seat next to him. And succeeding. "I would prefer to sit in the back," she said flatly.

Tough. He only mouthed the word, but the pat on her fanny was very close to a push, and he grinned suddenly. *I'm proud of you,* he mouthed again.

Was that supposed to make sense? The man was crazier than she was, and her hands were still shaking. Somewhere in the back of her head she felt a terrible ache, sudden and sharp, taunting her with the memory of failing Gram whom she loved so very much—failing her by failing to be assertive, and endlessly strong, and a thousand other things she'd expected of herself . . . and never seemed to be.

Hart started the engine. As soon as they were on the road, Marie leaned over the front seat, and that seductive, teasing note she'd used for Hart was gone. This was strictly Marie to Bree. "Look, darling, we've been together forever. You can't just give up your work on a whim; you've got more sense than that. When you've thought this through—"

"I've thought it through. I'm sure in the past decade at least half of all women have thought it through. *Fulfillment's* the word. The media are trumpeting it. You'll be fulfilled if you're successful in your career, and you're a failure if you can't manage it all—house and job and husband and children to boot." Bree twisted around to offer Marie a stony glare. "Hogwash. It means trying to please everyone and going nuts in the process."

Marie sat back in her seat. "You're not," she said stiffly, "yourself."

That was certainly true. Knife spears were lancing in and around her temples; she was trembling like a leaf in the wind, and she was imagining that Hart had just winked at her, when he was clearly facing the road. Furthermore, she never... yelled. Much less at Marie, who'd come all this way to see her... only to be treated uncivilly?

Silence stretched in the car like a taut rubber band. Hart reached over, flicked on a tape, and classical guitar music filled that silence. She felt his eyes on her as clearly as she felt his hand reach for her thigh. She pushed the hand away. Like a fool, she wanted nothing more than to reach out to him, to be enfolded and protected and warmed... but again to turn to Hart out of need? He probably considered her a three-day wonder, the one woman in a million who didn't instantly throw herself at his feet; regardless, she wasn't his responsibility. She wasn't anyone's. Just her own.

Within a half-hour, Hart's headlights gleamed on Marie's rental car, which was parked by the cabin. They all rushed from Hart's blue New Yorker at the same time.

"Bree?" Marie straightened the collar of her dress, standing in the darkness.

Bree suddenly stretched her hands out, meeting Marie halfway. "I apologize if I sounded rude, and I'm sorry you came all this way for nothing," she said quietly.

"You can't be sure—"

"I'm very sure." Without a glance at Hart, Bree whirled toward the cabin. Inside. If she could just get inside . . . Nightmare shadows were swallowing her up, none of them real, just something in her head. She had to be alone.

Escape didn't prove that easy. As she walked toward the porch of her cabin, she heard Marie's car sputter and cough, and then die. Without turning around, she heard Hart offer to take a turn at starting the rental car. It wouldn't. She heard Marie say something in a panicked flutter, then Hart's blunt, "I'll put you on that plane. Believe me," which effectively let Bree off the hook. She couldn't conceivably cope with another hour of Marie's company. She really couldn't conceivably cope with anything for a little while. Her hand grasped the doorknob, and suddenly Hart was there, whirling her to face him on the dark porch.

"What the hell's come over you?" he said furiously.

That fury seemed to come out of nowhere. She stared at him blankly.

"You were doing damned fine," he hissed. "The broad's like dynamite with a constantly lit fuse. When I think of you working for her day after day—never mind." Hart's jaws clamped together. "The point is that you should be giving a victory cheer, and instead you're having a silent temper tantrum. What is happening?"

"*Nothing* is happening. Enjoy your ride to the airport," Bree said brightly.

Hart jammed his hands in his pockets. "For two cents, I'd take you over my knee."

"You'd have two black eyes first."

"I'll take the black eyes," he growled. "You just be here when I get back."

"I won't wait up," she said pleasantly. "Marie will

undoubtedly keep you busy, but then, you're outstanding at handling lit fuses."

Those cold blue of his eyes amazingly took on fire. "Make that one cent. *After* you tell me what you meant by that crack."

Marie called out. Hart turned his head for an instant, and Bree slipped inside the cabin and closed the door.

It wasn't hard to find her sleeping bag, but her tennis shoes were buried in the back of the wardrobe, and then there was the search for a flashlight with working batteries. Bree had no intention of being there when Hart returned.

Outside, she stumbled pell-mell toward the woods, quickly discovering that flashlights weren't very effective against a night as dark as black velvet. In time, she made it to the pond. Clouds wisped across the crescent moon, and the water was like a still, charcoal mirror. The stone shoreline was not the most comfortable of sites on which to lay out a sleeping bag.

Keep moving, Bree. Everything will be fine if you just keep moving . . . A mosquito buzzed in front of her nose; Bree swatted it as she backtracked to the forest's edge. The ground was a little damp, but once she'd tossed away a few branches and twigs, it wasn't an unbearably rough mattress. She stretched out the sleeping bag, slapped another mosquito, slipped off her jeans and tennis shoes in a record three seconds, and zipped herself in up to her throat.

About then her lungs took in one wretched breath after another. She felt like an utter fool. Ungratefully spouting off to Marie, who'd come such a long way to see her, running off as if ghosts were chasing her, snapping at Hart . . . and she really knew why he'd been glaring at her all evening. Marie might not have known it, but she'd been describing Bree as a woman who jumped before

anyone even told her how high. Hart had contempt for
that kind of woman.

She didn't blame him; so did she.

Her head felt as if it were coming off. Wearily, Bree
closed her eyes and curled up in a ball.

The nightmare came back in the clouded mists of
sleep. It started as it always had, with Bree guiding Gram
through the stores, talking her out of carrying her packages, laughing as she ran to get the car. Then the dream
turned into a nightmare . . . but this time there was no
screaming siren. Before she felt crushed under the weight
of guilt and helplessness, Bree awoke to a predawn world
and utter quiet.

Silent tears streamed down her cheeks. She curled up
inside the sleeping bag, folded her arms around her knees,
and cried, rocking herself back and forth. Aching grief
surrounded her, inside and out. The tears she'd never
allowed before came pouring out, like a flood, an open
faucet, a bottomless well.

Up to this moment, she'd refused to accept the fact
that Gram was gone. She'd tried so hard to believe that
if she'd done something else, behaved in some different
way on that cold winter's day, that Gram would still be
alive. Always, that was the nightmare. She'd take a thousand nightmares rather than the loss. Grief filled her up
and was released in an explosion . . . an explosion of painful sobs. Yet the tower of guilt crumbled, and kept on
crumbling.

So much pain . . . but this time it hadn't been guilt for
Gram, but the loss for herself. Dozens of people had
loved and been loved by Bree, but only Gram had always
understood the things no one else could grasp, the silly
dreams and hopes she knew she couldn't fulfill. Gram
always believed she could. When Gram had died, Bree
felt in some terrible way that she'd failed her, but Gram
hadn't died because Bree had failed to save her. Gram

was a very old woman with a failing heart, and she had
died almost instantly on a cold February day.

Tears kept coming, choking her silently now. Maybe
that was the worst, knowing that change was happening
inside her; that the process of learning to believe in dreams
again was slow and not at all easy. It was happening,
but Gram was no longer there to share it. Gram was
gone . . .

"Damn you, Bree."

Her head jerked up. Instinctively, she cringed under
the single harsh beam of flashlight in her eyes, but the
light was quickly diverted to the ground. She had one
brief glimpse of his face, all dark shadows on granite
planes, midnight-blue eyes haunted with anxiety, before
Hart swooped down on her like a great offended bear.

He tossed some mosquito netting over her and tossed
the flashlight aside before gathering her up, sleeping bag
and all. His entire body was trying unsuccessfully to
transform itself into a blanket, wrapping her up, covering
her, securing her to his warmth.

She was still crying, and fighting very hard to stop.
He sat down, still holding her; she made a frantic movement to rise, and had her face gently pushed into his
chest for her trouble. "This time you're getting it all out,
Bree, and you'll do it right now."

He sounded so much like . . . Hart. A born bully, Hart,
with a low, soothing baritone and huge, warm arms that
wouldn't let her go. How could she fight that? The way
he murmured to her, you'd think it was perfectly all right
to cry, to release the last of a lonely grief, to let it all
go. The torrent of tears finally faded to a steady drip,
drip, drip, and an embarrassing occasional hiccup.

"Better?"

She nodded.

He didn't start scolding until she was ready to be
mopped up, half with a handkerchief and half with kisses.
"You realize how many hours I had to spend roaming

around looking for you? Couldn't you have just once, just *once,* accepted a little help from someone without trying to take the whole damn world on your shoulders?"

Exhausted, Bree said quietly, "I'm fine, Hart. Really, I've always been fine. I never needed a caretaker before, and I don't need one now. You never had to—"

"No, I didn't *have* to." Hart pressed one swift, fierce kiss on her mouth before lifting his head to glare at her. "Since you didn't take your car, I figured you had to be camping out somewhere, but I *didn't* figure you'd pick a mosquito haven." He slapped irritably at his neck before fumbling with the rough white netting between them. "Actually, I did figure it, having very few options at this time of year."

In a silent whoosh, Bree was suddenly buried in a tangle of mosquito netting. That wouldn't have been so bad if Hart weren't trying to bury himself with her. "Now just be a patient for a minute, Bree."

Patient? It was like tussling with a wild animal in the middle of the night. He leaned forward, the weight of his thigh nearly crushing her. She got a mouthful of mosquito netting when she tried to protest; vaguely she heard the zipper of her sleeping bag being pulled down, and then he was trying to tug her out of it as if she were a sack of potatoes. "If you'd sit *still* for a minute..." he growled at her impatiently.

It was hard to stay miserable when she was in so much danger of smothering. *"What* are you trying to do besides kill me?"

"There." His voice reeking with satisfaction, Hart finished his contortions. Sitting cross-legged, using his head for the mosquito-netting tent pole, he wrangled Bree to his lap and more or less covered her with her sleeping bag for warmth. What wasn't covered by her sleeping bag had certainly been covered by him. His arms were wrapped so tightly around her she could barely breathe.

His lips pressed, hard, on her forehead, then in her hair. "I knew it was going to happen tonight," he whispered.

"What?" He felt . . . disastrously good. Her cheek lay against the beat of his heart, and the longer he held her, the more his warmth filled up the terrible yawning hollow that the tears had drained. She felt comforted when she shouldn't have felt comforted at all. It was past time she handled her own problems, stopped leaning on a man who'd upset her entire life and was a little too good with women besides. She tried to sneak a hand up to rub away the last of the tears from her cheeks, and found Hart's hand already there.

The pads of his thumbs, very gently, brushed away the final glistening of salty sparkle beneath her eyes. "You had to break down sometime," he said quietly. "It just couldn't keep going on. Don't you think it's time you told me about it?"

She shook her head no, and in response, felt a scolding trail of kisses whisper through her hair.

"Tell me." More kisses tracked down the side of her cheek and then back into her hair again. "I've had enough of guessing, and hearing it secondhand. Your father said something about your grandmother dying, and I milked Marie for every other clue I could get, but what is all this business about your 'not being yourself right now'? I don't know who this 'yourself' is supposed to be, but the Bree I know is a most appealing, extremely sensitive, richly complex woman. She's a little stubborn." He tacked a kiss just behind her ear. "She's inclined to take other people a little too seriously. She looks a little like a drowned rat when she pulls back her hair." He centered another kiss on her chin. That one lingered. "Dammit, Bree. Let me help you."

His arms tightened around her when she tried to get up. Hart could be unforgivably stubborn. After a time, she leaned her cheek against his chest and sighed irritably.

The mosquito netting made a cocoon around the two of them; outside was darkness, the damp loneliness of almost dawn.

It seemed forever before she found her voice again, a voice that tried to sound light and casual. "My grandmother was just . . . so special. I've had people I loved and who loved me all my life, Hart—it's not as though I was ever deprived, but with Gram . . . she was a kindred spirit. There could never be anyone like her again. She embraced life every morning, every minute of the day; she could make you believe in rainbows . . ." Bree's voice trailed off, a lump in her throat again.

"And you loved her." Hart's fingers started to comb slowly through her hair, sifting through it, soothing it.

"I loved her; I respected her; I wanted to be like her. She always said I was; but it wasn't true. And when she died . . . something happened. I'm still not sure whether I felt it was Gram I failed, or myself. It seemed part and parcel of the same thing. Everything I'd always valued didn't seem important anymore. I wanted that joy of life Gram had; I wanted to go after it . . ." Bree hesitated and then smiled wryly, raising her eyes to Hart's. "So I dropped a perfectly secure job; I did a dear John on my fiancé, I worried my parents half to death; I took off—hardly mature, responsible actions, now, were they?"

"I think," Hart said gravely, "that in a sense those were very responsible actions."

"Hart, your judgment is just not a help. You're as off the wall as I am," she whispered, and received a lopsided grin in reply.

"Now you listen. It isn't crazy to go after what you want in life; it's crazy *not* to. And as for your grandmother . . ." Hart shifted, trying to make a space for both of them to lie down. "You never disappointed her, Bree. I don't need to have known her to be very sure of that. And whether you realize it or not, you've got the fighting instincts of a pro. I should know." Once he'd settled her on his arm, he hesitated, leaning over her, and started restlessly sifting his fingers through her hair again.

"You should know," Bree agreed.

"Sun's coming up," Hart remarked.

"I noticed." Fingers of gray had stolen into the darkness. She could make out Hart's face, the shadows and planes, the dark softness in his eyes.

"You look like hell when you've been crying, you know. Your face is all splotchy."

"Thanks so much. I can always count on you to say the most complimentary—"

"Marry me, Bree."

A robin twittered somewhere. Probably her imagination, Bree thought in a rush. When one started hearing voices, heaven knew how fast the rest of the mind could crack.

Chapter Twelve

BREE SHOOK HER HEAD with a nervous little laugh. "First I lost my voice, and now my hearing seems to be going. I could have sworn you just said—"

"Marry me."

Stunned, Bree tried to search his face in the dim light, but Hart's eyes seemed to be shuttered beneath thick dark lashes. "You're not serious," she said.

"Of course I'm serious. You already know I love you. Whether you like it or not, you're in love with me. I don't really see that we have any other choice."

"Hart." Maybe he was joking. Of course he was joking. But being Hart, he *would* give her a really wretched demonstration of his sick humor when her emotions were in an upheaval and she couldn't think straight. And that "You already know I love you" hurt. It hadn't occurred to her before how badly she wanted to hear those words . . . but not said lightly, or accompanied by an offer of marriage.

Bree kicked out at the mosquito netting, and after thoroughly tangling herself in the white cloth managed to twist free and stand up. Hart bunched the cloth into a huge white pillow and leaned back against it, watching her. She couldn't figure out the strange tension that seemed to grip his features; Hart was never tense. His voice was certainly as teasing as ever as he remarked, "You adore me, you know."

"You're full of peanuts. And—among *other* things— you just spent an entire dinner totally absorbed in another woman. Not to mention the beauties I saw bustling around your place like a harem of slaves."

Astonishment shone from his eyes. "What on earth are you talking about? *What* harem?"

"Hart," Bree said lowly, "you've had more women helping you fix up your place than a hive has hornets, and most of them looked like jailbait."

A faint smile creased his cheeks. "Because they are."

"Wonderful."

"Reninger has six granddaughters. I told you about him—the man I went to dinner with, the night we . . . uh—"

"I remember," she said stiffly.

"They've been friends of the family for years; I always see them when I'm on vacation." He added mildly, "I diapered most of the girls a few years back."

"They *certainly* haven't needed that recently."

"Beauties," Hart agreed. "The two oldest are twins, seventeen, and they both definitely fill out a bikini. Nubile or not, I usually manage to control myself where children are concerned. And hard as it is to believe, I'm just too old to take on two at a time, much less six. Because most of the time they come *en masse*—"

"All right, Hart." Bree could feel a flush of embarrassment heating her cheeks.

"Actually, they always help me set up house when I come here on vacation. And my mom usually houses the whole Reninger troop for a few weeks in August—"

"I get the picture," Bree muttered uncomfortably.

"Sure?" Hart asked dryly.

"*Very* sure."

"And as for my absorption in Marie over dinner, my sweet nitwit, I wouldn't have *had* to pump her if you'd been a little less stingy talking about yourself. Getting information out of you is like pumping a dry well. But if you read any more than that into the attention I gave Marie, I'm going to be insulted. I happen to have," he informed her, "much better taste in women."

He didn't give her much chance to answer before his tone changed. The lightness was suddenly gone, and his eyes held a quiet watchfulness as his finger traced her cheek. "Bree," he said quietly, "you persist in imagining racy scenes in my background. I'm not saying I haven't been around, but fidelity happens to be one of those old-fashioned values I could never quite shake. You'll be stuck keeping me happy, honey, don't doubt it. And I certainly don't plan on giving you any reason to look elsewhere for someone to keep you satisfied in bed."

Flushed and nervous, Bree raked a hand through her hair. She suddenly knew he was serious, and the old Bree sneaked to the surface, the Bree who was terribly afraid of foundering in unfamiliar waters. "Hart," she said haltingly, "you don't *marry* someone just because you love them. There have to be other reasons. Sane, rational reasons. Sensible reasons."

He was silent.

"We argue all the time," she reminded him.

He said nothing.

"We haven't known each other very long. We don't have anything in common. I don't even know where we'd live!"

Still he said nothing.

"And my life is a mess—haven't you been listening? I—"

"Yes, I've been listening," Hart interrupted quietly, "but I've never seen your life as a mess, Bree. All I saw was that you'd taken a turning you didn't like and were backtracking toward a different path. Perhaps," he added lightly, "I misunderstood a great deal. Because I never much gave a damn where we'd live. Or about 'sane, rational reasons,' either." He sat up, ducking his head for a moment, and when he raised it there was a lazy grin on his face, typically Hart, swiftly erasing any hint of an earlier emotional turmoil. "You can put your smile back on, red. Nobody's upset. And anyway," he said firmly, "it's time for breakfast."

He pulled her to her feet, and for a moment Bree stood absolutely still. Then she reached for her jeans and tennis shoes. She'd hurt him. She'd rather break all four limbs than ever hurt Hart. She'd *never* meant to be insensitive; she'd tried to treat the subject of marriage lightly because Hart treated *everything* lightly . . . but not this. She could see from the quickly masked vulnerability in his eyes that he'd simply known no other way to ask her . . . or that maybe she'd never given him much of a chance.

"Cornflakes at your place or mine?" Hart's teasing grin was the same, only his eyes looked different. Hollow and weary.

"Hart—"

"Yours. Then you'll get stuck with the cleanup. Come on, lady." He gathered up her sleeping bag and the netting, motioned her to hurry up tying her shoes, and then flung an arm loosely across her shoulders as they started from the woods, all devil-may-care. "We're going to make wine today," he said swiftly.

"Wine?" There was such a huge lump in her throat that she could barely talk. Her hands were trembling. Hart *loved* her. Could he really? He'd already dropped the subject as if it had never been mentioned. Bree didn't want to drop it, but she didn't have the least idea how to reopen the door she'd just closed in his face.

Hart stopped to turn and chuck her under the chin. Very gravely, he turned up one corner of her mouth and then the other as if he could order up a smile. "Cherry wine," he continued. "There's no reasons to look all upset. We're going to have a very good time. I picked up an antique press a few days ago, and I want to put it to use."

Bree surfaced, forcing the smile he was so insistent

she wear. She searched his eyes and found there only a shuttered determination that she didn't know how to handle. Vaguely, her mind registered what he'd been talking about. "Hart, don't be an idiot. Where on earth are you going to find cherries at this time of year?"

"I'll get the cherries. And the sugar and the yeast. All you have to do is provide the brawn, honey."

He wasn't joking. Three hours later, Bree's yard looked like a winery. A sticky winery. Hart had brought down two lawn chairs from his place. And two wooden barrels. And a hundred pounds of cherries.

The wine press stood in the center of the mess, an innocent-looking contraption. One poured a bowl of cherries into the machine and turned the crank, and *voilà*, cherry juice was supposed to stream out into the waiting sterile bowl, and the pits and cherry skins were all supposed to remain inside.

It wasn't working. The pits and cherries remained inside, just as the cherry-press inventor had intended. But most of the cherry juice, as far as Bree could tell, was all over her. Wearing a fresh pair of white jeans— definitely a foolish choice of attire—and black halter top, she whipped back her hair with the side of her wrist and glared at Hart.

"How did you miraculously produce that clean white shirt?"

He grinned at her, his fingers still buttoning the shirt. "I picked up a pile of shirts from the local laundry yesterday, and left them in my car. And since the other shirt seemed to be a little sticky—"

"*Very* little," Bree said ominously.

"You're obviously much better than this than I am."

"The question is how I let you talk me into this to begin with."

"I must have asked you real nice?" Hart peered down into the bowl, batting aimlessly at a few buzzing bees that had grown interested in the sweet project. "Think of the delicious brew we'll have later on," he coaxed. "Look, I'll take another turn—"

"You will *not*." The last time he'd had a round at the cranking job, cherry juice had ended up all over the lawn. He'd been banished to the lawn chair. Wearing a pair of cutoffs and now a fresh white shirt, he barely looked as though he'd been in the first skirmish, much less the war.

"Bree—"

She gave him a suspicious look. The last of three. It would be just like him to act useless just to get out of doing any serious work. She knew Hart.

And her heart was so damned full of love for him that she was very close to crying, and had been all day. Hart would get her involved in some asinine activity simply to get her mind off her troubles. He'd done it before. She was only beginning to realize how often. "Take off your shirt," she ordered briskly.

"My shirt? Why?"

"Just give it here. This isn't working. We've used fifty pounds of cherries, and at best, we've got a cup of potential wine. If you're going to do something old-fashioned, Hart, you've got to do it right. Strip," she ordered flatly.

"Honey, if you're in the mood, all you have to do is say so." Slowly, Hart unbuttoned his shirt, grinning at her.

"Dream on." He was going too slowly; she positioned herself in front of him and unbuttoned the shirt herself. The last button didn't want to undo, probably because her heart had decided to suddenly go manic. His denim cutoffs were so old they were more white than blue; they fit snugly on his hips and snugly on the . . . front of him. Sunlight climbed all over his chest. That close, Hart smelled like Hart, that definitive man smell, creating wanton thoughts and vagrant wishes and a bold, blatant ache in Bree that utterly, totally distracted her.

Hart's fingers abruptly tickled under her chin. "You want me to lick off all that cherry juice?" he murmured. "I'll bet you have it all over you, Bree. It's dribbled down your shirt—"

She flushed. "It hasn't either." Her fingers all but tore the shirt from his shoulders. "Now, into the cabin you go. I want clean feet. *Sterile* feet. And bring out the big flat pan in the cupboard by the stove. We're going to crush the cherries the French way, Mr. Manning—"

It was her turn to sit back in the lawn chair with a glass of lemonade. She wrapped some cherries in the clean white shirt; Hart's job was to stomp them until he'd squeezed the juice out into the pan.

"If you don't stop laughing—" he warned.

She couldn't stop. She wasn't in the mood to laugh; she was still in the mood to cry, but he looked so silly. He started to whistle the theme from *Zorba the Greek*, and that didn't help. Nothing helped. She felt her mood lighten in spite of herself. She kept watching Hart for the least sign that he was upset or even that he was willing to talk again, but the minute he felt her eyes on him he'd say something insulting, and then she'd insult him back, and then they'd be laughing again . . .

It was an hour later before they had enough cherry juice to pour into the crocks, and then it was simply a matter of adding sugar and yeast. Except that Hart poured in too much sugar. Bree stood back for the torrent of muttered four-letter words that followed.

"Which couldn't matter less," she scolded him. "You don't think anyone would be crazy enough to drink this?"

"I've got news. You're drinking at least half," Hart said flatly.

"Only if there's a hospital nearby."

"Look, the brewing process will destroy any germs—"

"*Hart*. There are undoubtedly *creatures* in that juice. We've drawn every insect from at least five hundred miles around. Between your feet and the bugs—"

"I suppose you think my feet will add an unpleasant taste?"

Hart sounded injured. Bree *felt* injured. Her cranking shoulder felt like a candidate for a sling; she was so physically tired she was dizzy—how many years was it since she'd had a full night's sleep, anyway?—and somewhere deep inside her, there was another ache.

Laughter suddenly died, for no reason at all. She lifted her head, and suddenly Hart's eyes were there, as midnight blue as when she'd first seen them, but different. Love was there. Hurt was there. A depth, an enigmatic softness, a blue sky turned into night.

And he was looking back at her. She could almost see what he did, an utterly bedraggled woman without makeup, cherry juice on her nose, a halter top clinging to her, red hair flowing in a curling tangle all around her; she *had* to have circles under her eyes ... but she felt beautiful, the way he looked at her. So incredibly beautiful ...

She wrenched her eyes away from his only because she heard a car, and even then the station wagon had pulled into the yard before she turned around.

The station wagon was familiar. So was the man who stepped out of it. Tall, dark, and attractive, he was dressed in a conservative summer-weight suit, his shirt crisp. He peeled off his sunglasses when he spotted her. "Bree?" He sounded unsure as he gave the bedraggled lady in the yard a quick once-over.

Helplessly, Bree whipped her gaze back to Hart, who had stood up. For a moment, he just looked weary, and then he turned an ironic smile on Bree. "Don't tell me," he said dryly. "The fiancé. I should have known the troops wouldn't stop with just two visits. The last of the battalion arriveth to take you back to sanity, is that it, Bree? And doesn't he look nice." Hart cast him another look. "A little tame for you, I would think, but still true-blue dependable."

Bree cast him a desperately unhappy look. "I broke my engagement, Hart. Before I met you. And I didn't ask him here—"

Hart wasn't paying attention. He was striding past her with an arm extended. Richard, to give him credit, didn't blink an eye at the sticky handshake, just offered Hart and then Bree a rather bewildered smile.

"Darling? I barely recognized you . . ."

Darling, nothing. Richard, would you please go away? Bree's heart moaned, but Hart was gathering up his shoes, picking up the mosquito netting from beside the chair. There was an I've-had-it air about him that frightened Bree.

"Bree? You're all right? You're talking now? Your parents said—"

"I'm fine. I . . . just a minute, would you?" Bree's eyes zipped away from Richard back to Hart. Dammit, he was striding out of the yard without another word. At a dead run, she caught up with him, snatching at his arm.

"Just *wait* a minute," she said heatedly.

Something was wrong with Hart's expression. The warmth was gone, replaced by a coolness that seemed impenetrable. He unhooked her hand from his arm and very softly brushed back a wisp of hair from her cheek. "There's nothing to wait for, Bree. There"—he cocked his head in Richard's direction—"is sane, rational marriage material if I've ever seen it. Exactly what I think you're looking for, honey. You'd better think things over pretty damn carefully before you reject him again."

"I—"

But Hart was heading for the woods, and Richard was coming toward her with a boyishly embarrassed expression.

"Bree? Did I interrupt something?"

Richard was attractive and kind and intelligent and good-natured. But at times he could be remarkably obtuse.

* * *

"The minute your parents told me you'd regained your speech, there was no question I was coming down. I never really believed you meant to end our engagement, Bree. You weren't yourself. Here, darling..."

Richard forked a sliver of prime rib onto her place, smiling at her. Moments before, he'd stolen a chunk of the veal cutlet she hadn't touched so far. It was an old habit between them, tasting each other's dinners when they were out. The kind of habit that defines the intimacy between two people.

Once upon a time, she'd thought those little habits could sustain the relationship. She picked at her food; there was very little point in eating it, since each bite made her ill. She hadn't felt she had any choice but to accept Richard's invitation to dinner; he'd meant too much to her, once upon a time, and like Marie, he'd come a very long distance to see her.

And Hart's cutting sarcasm had hurt. Richard wasn't "nice" as in boring; he was "nice" as in very good man. As the waitress cleared the table and poured coffee, he smiled at her across the table. The smile was an affectionate, don't-worry, everything's-going-to-be-fine smile. Richard was not only a good man; he was soothing to be around and always had been.

Totally unlike Hart.

"Your vacation's done you good, Bree," Richard said quietly. "You're brown, and you don't look nearly so tired."

"Thank you." Bree carefully stirred two spoonfuls of sugar into her coffee and then stared down at it. She never took sugar. Taking a breath, she faced Richard's soft brown eyes. "I wish you had told me ahead of time that you were coming—"

"I could have wired," he agreed. "But I was eager to see you. I don't want to push you into anything, Bree, but I came to return something to you." He took a small, square box from his pocket and set it gently on the table.

Bree recognized the ring box and remembered well the night he'd given it to her. He'd been so terribly nervous; Richard abhorred emotional scenes, and she'd tried to make it easier for him. He'd set it up with champagne and soft lights, and she'd felt like saying no such fuss was necessary. They'd both known where the relationship was going; both had cautiously tested the way for months. They'd discussed their favorite foods, their common interests, how many children they wanted, what kind of house they wanted to live in.

She remembered that strange instant of panic when she'd first opened the box to that diamond solitaire, all alone in its fourteen-karat-gold setting. She'd felt the crazy sensation that she was pinning herself down to a lifetime of being alone in a misleadingly safe and beautiful setting, but she'd pushed the sensation aside and kissed him.

But that was how she'd looked at things then. Safety had seemed so important. One didn't make major decisions about one's life based on crazy, wild, romantic, combustible feelings...

Dammit. What was Hart doing now?

"Darling?" Richard's voice was coaxing, very gentle.

Bree felt like brushing back that shock of dark hair from his forehead as she would for a child. "I can't take the ring back," she said softly. "It's not because I don't care for you. I always did and I always will, and I wish you the absolute best. But it wouldn't work, Richard, not the right way. I really can't be the wife you truly want—"

"Of course you can." Richard leaned forward, his dark eyes as soft as a spaniel's. "Please, Bree. Listen to me. We have absolutely everything in common. I tried to understand your wanting a period of time alone down here—and I'll still try to understand, if you want more time to yourself. I waited to come because I didn't want to upset or push you, but if you want me to wait a little longer . . ."

No, Bree thought wretchedly. You dear man, you would never have pushed me.

Richard would have let her go on not talking; Richard would have agreed to a vacation in the Arctic if she'd asked; Richard would have let her hibernate for a year if she'd wanted to. Richard didn't like arguments and had always had the endearing quality of wanting to please. So unlike Hart. Hart took hearts and shredded them up in his free time. And if she'd tried an itty-bitty hibernating nap with Hart, he'd have kicked her out of bed . . . well, maybe not *bed* . . . but he'd certainly have shouted at her to get on with her life. There was just no rest with Hart. He was unsettling and upsetting . . .

And she was in a terrible hurry to get back to him.

Bree gently pushed the ring box toward Richard, hating the hurt in his eyes, hating herself for being the cause of it. "Time won't change things," she said gently. "Please accept that. I can't take it back, Richard, and I'm terribly sorry I've hurt you—"

"Now, Bree. Let's talk about this," he insisted.

One of Richard's few faults was that he had *such* a thick skin. Helplessly, Bree watched the waitress serve a second cup of coffee and then a third. Richard started to talk computers, knowing from time-honored habit that shoptalk inevitably calmed her down.

She tried to listen, feeling she owed him that much. She tried to smile, and her mind tried frantically to stop thinking about Hart. It didn't work. The only thing in her head was how he'd walked off in such a final way. Maybe he was packing to leave now. It was like him, to sever a relationship as quickly as he'd established it. He wasn't a patient man. He was an irrational man, with a thousand really maddening qualities. He expected people to change overnight. He had no tolerance at all for people who didn't shout about what they wanted from life, who didn't go after it, who didn't run full speed after what made them happy . . .

" . . . I can understand your not wanting to work with Marie. I always thought she gave you the short end of the stick, Bree. There's an opening in the company I work for; I know I could get you in, and—"

"Richard?" Bree interrupted quietly. She looked him square in the eye, stopped trying to smile, and took a deep breath. Being nice was so much . . . nicer. It was just a pity that being nice didn't always work. *"No,"* she said simply.

Silence echoed across the table for a good sixty seconds. Bree finally broke it by reaching down to pick up her purse.

Chapter Thirteen

As soon as Richard's car left the driveway, Bree flew
into the cabin and up the loft stairs, stripping off the
yellow cotton frock she'd worn for dinner. She tossed
on the bed, in rapid succession, her dress, stockings,
slip, and underpants. Stripped down to bare skin, she
raced back downstairs, leaped gingerly onto the dry sink,
and started pumping in water. There was no time to take
a bath in the pond. She was in too much of a hurry.

Maybe he was already gone. Or maybe he was just
out. Or maybe he was picking up another woman somewhere. Or maybe...

Lowering her dripping feet to the floor, she rubbed
her skin dry with a towel and flew back up the stairs
again. Tugging open the wardrobe, she thumbed through
the hangers impatiently, finding absolutely nothing with
any seductive potential. She'd packed for solitary cottage
living, not come-hither nonsense. And you shouldn't be
racing; you should be feeling thoroughly guilty over
Richard, she told herself severely, as she lifted out a stark
white silk blouse, wrinkled her nose, and let the blouse
fall to the floor.

She did feel guilty, actually. She'd shared a great deal
with Richard, and she cared for him and she was mis-
erably sorry he'd traveled so far for nothing. But con-
tinuing to sit and listen to him wasn't going to lessen his
hurt and it wasn't going to change her feelings. Besides,

whether he knew it or not, she would have made him
terribly unhappy. A good man deserved a good woman.

She just wasn't that eternally good Bree anymore. She
was a most imperfect Bree, a lady willing to throw away
all common sense for the love of a most imperfect man.
A man who made her feel terribly alive every second
she was with him. A man who was a fibber and a fraud
and a little bit of a bully and who regularly insulted her
and who was far too attractive to other women . . .

Really, that she knew all his faults and didn't care had
to be either a sign of mental degeneration or an extreme
case of a love worth shouting for.

Reaching for a mint-green camisole, she held it up to
the mirror and decided Hart would like it . . . especially
if she wore it braless. The straps were little more than
satin ribbons, the bodice skimmed the tops of her breasts,
and when she bought it, she hadn't been absolutely positive whether it was a top or underwear.

Hart *had* to like it.

The mint-green short shorts weren't exactly seductive,
but she was limited by the wardrobe at hand. At least
they showed off her brown legs . . . Bending close to the
crooked mirror in the corner, she lavished on mascara,
eye shadow, and her most delectable perfume. On second
thought, she brushed on a quick layer of blusher. On
third thought, she added a little lip gloss. Her hair . . .
her hair was a wreck, weaving every which way in determined auburn waves. One wave, when she worked
with it, formed a seductive curl over one eye. Quitting
while she was ahead, she raced downstairs.

And back up again for her shoes.

And down again. Panting in the doorway, she took in
a steadily falling dusk and started off for the woods. Take
the car, a small voice in her head sensibly reminded her.
But it really would be faster to walk through the woods,
if she could just find those steps Hart had told her about.

The rain the day before seemed to have washed down

the sky. The air was clear, the night hot, and a yellow moon was rising over the hills. In that hush of evening, the scent of trillium and rhododendron flooded the stillness, a sweet, potent perfume that stirred her senses. *Live,* had always been Gram's message. *Live. Don't waste even seconds; feel everything you can possibly feel . . .*

It was there, inside her. The potential to love she had never felt before, the potential to give and hurt and laugh with sheer joy and share and, yes, fight for her right to those things.

Her fingers trembled suddenly, pushing through the undergrowth. Fighting *for* Hart was very different from fighting *with* him. What if . . . She stumbled over a halfburied stone and, muttering a few violent imprecations, decided to let the "what if's" take a hike. Hart was stuck with her, whether he knew it or not. She might have had a screw loose originally, but he had convinced her that safety and sanity weren't a pair, that something as nebulous as love could be unshakable and strong.

It grew dark faster than was fair. At least too fast for her to find the blasted steps. If she hadn't been in such an impulsive rush, she would have taken the car. She'd been in an impulsive rush to *something* ever since she'd met the wretched man. And the bramble patch she walked into was worse than the one she'd tangled with the other night. One branch tried to take off with her hair, and another picked at her camisole. Tiny branches whipped her bare legs, and all of them were harboring huge, fluttering moths or nasty little mosquitoes.

By the time she reached the top of the ravine, Bree was hot, miserable, and distinctly unseductive-looking. She was also in a rage. Her mascara had run; one camisole strap was dangling. She had a splotch of mud on the seat of her shorts, and dirt was itching between her toes. Hart's fault. Everything was Hart's fault.

If that judgment wasn't rational, it covered up a terrible anxiety fairly well. He'd said he loved her just that

morning. He'd said he wanted to marry her. It was just
... when he'd walked away, her heart had picked up
the cadence of fear, and she hadn't been able to lose it
since. Hart wasn't the kind to wait around. And she'd
hurt him. She hadn't told him she loved him back, and
he was still under the stupid impression that he was a
free man. Hart wasn't safe walking around loose. She
ought to know.

Climbing onto his patio, she whisked what dirt she
could off her shorts and ran frenetic fingers through her
hair. Irritably, she kicked off her sandals and brushed her
feet on his doormat so that they were at least reasonably
clean. Lifting her chin then, she peered through the glass
door, and when she saw nothing, frowned and arched a
palm over her eyes to see in better.

A single light was on in his living room. The unpacking mess had been cleared up. A pair of tennies and
a pair of dress shoes were lying on the floor, which gave
her at least a reasonable expectation that he hadn't skipped
town. She raised her knuckles to the glass, then hesitated.

Knocking was one of life's basic courtesies, request-
ing permission to enter. Courtesy suddenly seemed terribly expensive, when it carried the risk that he just might
not willingly give her that permission. Determinedly, she
slid open the door and called out a tentative "Hart?"

There was no answer. She stepped in. "Hart?" Rub-
bing her forearm with her other hand, she hesitated again.
His house was cool; she felt a chill steal up her spine.
Too cool, too quiet.

Wandering forward, she poked her head in the kitchen
but found nothing except a predictable sinkful of dishes
and the remains of a TV dinner. She sighed irritably. So
he wasn't much of a housekeeper, on top of everything
else. Thanks, God. I had to fall for one of the uncivilized
ones.

She tiptoed down the hall, feeling like an intruder.

Had he already written her off? She couldn't bear the thought.

"Hart?" she whispered at his bedroom door, and then pushed it open a little. He wasn't there. The bed was made, though, giving her slight cause for rejoicing as to his potential for being domesticated. If she'd felt like rejoicing. She felt like bursting into tears. *Too late, too late, too late,* her heart echoed. She recalled all the times he had battled past her armor, the times he'd just been there for her, the times he'd brought out a passion that she would never have believed she had, the times he'd forced her to say out loud what she wanted, to face things she'd thought were hard. They weren't so hard. Losing him—that was the only thing in life she couldn't bear. But maybe he'd just had enough of battling, and she couldn't blame him.

Despair was trying to seep into her heart. She forced herself to walk the rest of the way down the hall and push open the door to a spare bedroom she hadn't seen before. She found boxes stacked to the ceiling but still no man with navy-blue eyes and a lion's mane of hair. Glumly, she paused at the bathroom, gave the door a token push, and then uttered a startled gasp.

The room was shadowed and dark. From inside, she heard a loud slosh of water that nearly scared her out of her wits, and then a giant surged up out of the darkness. Grabbing the door handle, she slammed it shut and leaned back against the opposite wall.

"Bree?"

"What the *devil* are you doing taking a bath in the dark?" she yelled. Her heart was beating like a rabbit's. Terrifying her like that—it was on the list of things she was never going to forgive him for.

"It wasn't dark a half-hour ago. You're welcome to come in." The baritone positively *exuded* lazy amusement.

"No, thank you." She slumped back against the wall, and then let gravity take over. Her back slid down until her bottom hit carpet, and she just sat there. Silence echoed up and down the hall ominously. "Hart?"

He didn't answer, but she could again hear water sloshing around in there. She bit at the nail of her little finger, looked at it disgustedly, and folded her arms across her chest. "I came to tell you a few things," she called out irritably. Great beginning, Bree. What did he think you came here for, a game of tiddlywinks? "Listen. I'm not going to do all the cooking and cleaning up, you know."

When there was no answer, she raised her voice a little. "And there are a few other things. I know that by some miracle you settled things with my dad, Hart, but it's got to go further than that. I want you to like each other . . . because of Christmas and babies, and all that kind of thing. And I don't have the least idea where you really live, but I'd just as soon we'd settle in Siberia. I can tell you right now I'm not going to put up with the way other women look at you." She gnawed at her lip. "And this bullying tendency of yours. I'm not saying I didn't occasionally give you cause, but if you think you're getting a pushover, Hart, you're going to be terribly disappointed."

She waited, but there was nothing. Suddenly, there wasn't even the sound of sloshing water. She bit at her fingernail again. "And you should computerize your business. The system you have is terribly inefficient—honestly, you should be ashamed of yourself. That's something I could do for you, Hart, but not full time. This will probably sound perfectly frivolous, but all my life I've secretly wanted to make perfumes. I've got to learn some chemistry, because I mean to create, produce, market . . . the whole bit. Does that sound crazy?" Her voice trailed off. She wasn't at all sure why she was rambling on about such ridiculous nonessentials.

"Are you listening?" she asked weakly.

He said nothing. She shook the finger on her left hand, having bitten the nail down to the quick. "Hart, I love you," she said helplessly to the closed door.

It opened as if by magic. Hart's hair was damp, and he'd wrapped a towel haphazardly around his hips, and he loomed over her like a big, blond, wet bear. The smile that wreathed his features bore no relationship to his thundering growl. "What the *hell* took you so long to get rid of him?"

"Richard?"

"Whoever." Hart scooped her up, ignoring her startled squeal. He was still wet. "I've been waiting for you for hours, you know." His mouth hovered over hers, homed in. And lifted again. "If you'd come much later, you would have found me halfway through a bottle of brandy."

"You mean apple juice."

"Honey, I mean *brandy*. And what happened to your eyes?"

"Nothing," she said tersely, well aware her three layers of mascara had smudged.

"You look like you've been through a war."

"Do I really need this?" she asked the ceiling absently, and found the ceiling falling a distance away as Hart released her. On an undulating wave, she hit the water bed.

Hart followed, a gleam in his eyes a brilliant as a sapphire's. One long leg swiftly looped over hers, pinning her, but the fingers that reached out to brush back her hair were neither playful nor rough, but infinitely tender. She looked into the mirrors of his eyes, they were that close, and she could see a beautiful, infinitely wanted, deeply loved woman inside them. Her heart slowed down for the first time in hours.

In fact, it went sluggish, as Hart's lips grazed her temples, then her nose, then her upper lip. His mouth sank down slowly, with exquisite patience. The kiss was soft and cherishing rather than sexual. Her fingers pushed back his damp, thick hair possessively. "Hart? Did you hear one word I said?" she whispered.

"I heard you. And I'll cook, Bree." Being Hart, with his particular mammary obsession, his eyes located the broken ribbon on her camisole before she'd noticed it herself. With very little effort, he broke the other ribbon strap and pulled the soft material down to her ribs. Only reluctantly did his eyes shift back to hers. "In the interests of honesty, I have to admit the only thing I can cook is spaghetti. But I buy terrific TV dinners."

He nuzzled first at her throat, tickling her with a softly lapping tongue, then trailed down to her breasts. He tasted first one and then the other before his eyes returned to hers. "I'll also make friends with your father," he promised gravely. "Frankly, I think we'll get along just fine. We both share a great many values—you being the first one. We both want to make you happy; we both love you. And if I'd come to my daughter's house and found a man's clothes strewn all over the yard, I would have killed him. Your father is a man of remarkable restraint."

"You think so?"

He rose a little to unbutton her shorts. He slid them down and off, tossing them over his shoulder. The camisole followed. Her underpants followed. His towel followed. When he looked back at her, he frowned, as if trying to recall his train of thought. "And I never intended to take over your life, you know. You were running away. You were just too damn good a lady to be running away. There's nothing criminal about needing a little help once in a while, and you were clearly trying to take the entire world on your shoulders, while I was going nuts trying to make you shift just a little of it to mine. I wanted you to need me," he said quietly.

"I did."

"You didn't." He shook his head, stretched out beside

her. "You're a strong lady, honey. You would have gotten there. You don't *need* anyone. But you can still make the choice to share what's hurting you, and it's a choice that's made from love. And I've forgotten," he murmured, "the rest of your terms."

So did she, for a while. Their bodies edged closer, in a slow, languid hello to each other. Bree closed her eyes, feeling love so strong that it almost hurt, and yet it felt so right. His skin warmed for her fingertips; her heart accelerated for his.

"Your computers," he murmured suddenly, and lifted his head.

"Pardon?"

"You're going to computerize my company. That's fine, too, Bree, but not as important as a lab for your perfumes. You'll need a lab, and you can either go back to school to learn chemistry, or we could hire you a chemist. Whatever you want, honey—but there was still something else."

She could think of nothing else. Fleetingly, she considered taking advantage of Hart while he was in such a meek, submissive mood. It undoubtedly wouldn't last long.

"I know what it was." Hart trailed a finger between her breasts, circling first one and then the other, and then rubbing a nipple back and forth between his fingers until it rose, aching, like a soft red berry.

"Hart..." She was beginning to hurt from wanting him. It wasn't so much the terrible surge of passion as the terrible surge of love. She wanted to be joined with him, part of him.

"I know what it was. Did I hear you say you loved me?" he whispered.

She smiled. "I love you."

"Didn't hear you."

"I love you, Hart."

"Honey, maybe if you'd shout it..."

She should have known it was too good to last. She poked a fingertip in his chest, and watched the man crash on his back as if hit by a bulldozer. Smiling, she scooted on top of him, pinning his legs with one of hers and, just as he had done to her, she leaned over him, her fingers gently combing back his hair. "I'm sure, Hart," she whispered. "Very sure that I know what I want, and that's you. In my life. For all of my life. But you'd better be just as sure, because you know darn well we're going to argue a great deal—"

"No, we won't."

"Yes, we wi—" She stopped, gave him a rueful look, and zoomed in for a kiss. "Do you think you could prove just once that you can take a few orders instead of handing them out?" she whispered.

"Certainly."

"Then put your arms around my neck."

He complied.

"And move your body, just a little . . ."

He did.

"Now make love to me, Hart."

Grinning, he whispered, "See if I ever argue with you again, Bree."

Second Chance at Love ®

___ 0-425-07769-1	FIRE BIRD #242 Jean Barrett	$1.95
___ 0-425-07770-5	DEAR ADAM #243 Jasmine Craig	$1.95
___ 0-425-07771-3	NOTORIOUS #244 Karen Keast	$2.25
___ 0-425-07772-1	UNDER HIS SPELL #245 Lee Williams	$2.25
___ 0-425-07773-X	INTRUDER'S KISS #246 Carole Buck	$2.25
___ 0-425-07774-8	LADY BE GOOD #247 Elissa Curry	$2.25
___ 0-425-07775-6	A CLASH OF WILLS #248 Lauren Fox	$2.25
___ 0-425-07776-4	SWEPT AWAY #249 Jacqueline Topaz	$2.25
___ 0-425-07975-9	PAGAN HEART #250 Francine Rivers	$2.25
___ 0-425-07976-7	WORDS OF ENDEARMENT #251 Helen Carter	$2.25
___ 0-425-07977-5	BRIEF ENCOUNTER #252 Aimée Duvall	$2.25
___ 0-425-07978-3	FOREVER EDEN #253 Christa Merlin	$2.25
___ 0-425-07979-1	STARDUST MELODY #254 Mary Haskell	$2.25
___ 0-425-07980-5	HEAVEN TO KISS #255 Charlotte Hines	$2.25
___ 0-425-08014-5	AIN'T MISBEHAVING #256 Jeanne Grant	$2.25
___ 0-425-08015-3	PROMISE ME RAINBOWS #257 Joan Lancaster	$2.25
___ 0-425-08016-1	RITES OF PASSION #258 Jacqueline Topaz	$2.25
___ 0-425-08017-X	ONE IN A MILLION #259 Lee Williams	$2.25
___ 0-425-08018-8	HEART OF GOLD #260 Liz Grady	$2.25
___ 0-425-08019-6	AT LONG LAST LOVE #261 Carole Buck	$2.25
___ 0-425-08150-8	EYE OF THE BEHOLDER #262 Kay Robbins	$2.25
___ 0-425-08151-6	GENTLEMAN AT HEART #263 Elissa Curry	$2.25
___ 0-425-08152-4	BY LOVE POSSESSED #264 Linda Barlow	$2.25
___ 0-425-08153-2	WILDFIRE #265 Kelly Adams	$2.25
___ 0-425-08154-0	PASSION'S DANCE #266 Lauren Fox	$2.25
___ 0-425-08155-9	VENETIAN SUNRISE #267 Kate Nevins	$2.25
___ 0-425-08199-0	THE STEELE TRAP #268 Betsy Osborne	$2.25
___ 0-425-08200-8	LOVE PLAY #269 Carole Buck	$2.25
___ 0-425-08201-6	CAN'T SAY NO #270 Jeanne Grant	$2.25
___ 0-425-08202-4	A LITTLE NIGHT MUSIC #271 Lee Williams	$2.25
___ 0-425-08203-2	A BIT OF DARING #272 Mary Haskell	$2.25
___ 0-425-08204-0	THIEF OF HEARTS #273 Jan Mathews	$2.25

Prices may be slightly higher in Canada.

Available at your local bookstore or return this form to:

SECOND CHANCE AT LOVE
Book Mailing Service
P.O. Box 690, Rockville Centre, NY 11571

Please send me the titles checked above. I enclose _____ Include 75¢ for postage and handling if one book is ordered; 25¢ per book for two or more not to exceed $1.75. California, Illinois, New York and Tennessee residents please add sales tax.

NAME _____

ADDRESS _____

CITY _____ STATE/ZIP _____

(allow six weeks for delivery)   SK-41b

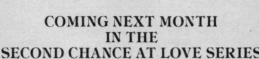

COMING NEXT MONTH
IN THE
SECOND CHANCE AT LOVE SERIES

QUESTIONNAIRE

1. How do you rate _____
                          (please print TITLE)
   ☐ excellent   ☐ good
   ☐ very good   ☐ fair   ☐ poor

2. How likely are you to purchase another book
   in this series?
   ☐ definitely would purchase
   ☐ probably would purchase
   ☐ probably would not purchase
   ☐ definitely would not purchase

3. How likely are you to purchase another book by
   this author?
   ☐ definitely would purchase
   ☐ probably would purchase
   ☐ probably would not purchase
   ☐ definitely would not purchase

4. How does this book compare to books in other
   contemporary romance lines?
   ☐ much better
   ☐ better
   ☐ about the same
   ☐ not as good
   ☐ definitely not as good

5. Why did you buy this book? (Check as many as apply)
   ☐ I have read other
      SECOND CHANCE AT LOVE romances
   ☐ friend's recommendation
   ☐ bookseller's recommendation
   ☐ art on the front cover
   ☐ description of the plot on the back cover
   ☐ book review I read
   ☐ other _____
      _____
      _____

(Continued...)

6. Please list your three favorite contemporary romance lines.

_____
_____

7. Please list your favorite authors of contemporary romance lines.

_____
_____
_____
_____
_____

8. How many SECOND CHANCE AT LOVE romances have you read? _____

9. How many series romances like SECOND CHANCE AT LOVE do you <u>read</u> each month? _____

10. How many series romances like SECOND CHANCE AT LOVE do you <u>buy</u> each month? _____

11. Mind telling your age?
    ☐ under 18
    ☐ 18 to 30
    ☐ 31 to 45
    ☐ over 45

☐ Please check if you'd like to receive our <u>free</u> SECOND CHANCE AT LOVE Newsletter.

We hope you'll share your other ideas about romances with us on an additional sheet and attach it securely to this questionnaire.

• •

Fill in your name and address below:
Name _____
Street Address _____
City _____ State _____ Zip _____

Please return this questionnaire to:
    SECOND CHANCE AT LOVE
    The Berkley Publishing Group
    200 Madison Avenue, New York, New York 10016